Ottilie's Obituary & Other Horror Stories

Daz Eek

Note From Author

Please note, as an English author, it's only natural for me to use UK spellings rather than those of American English, like 'colour' instead of 'color', for example. I hope you enjoy the stories!

Buy directly from Daz Eek at https://dazeek.com/.

Contents

Samuel Scarecrow 1

She's Jackie O'Leary 5

Hard Times in —s 11

For Alymer 13

Painted Tin Soldiers 46

Back at the Old House 53

Sacrifices 56

Ottilie's Obituary 60

Also by Daz Eek 75

Samuel Scarecrow

It's time for the reading of the annual scarecrow report, and so we all march down from our house to the bottom field—that's Mom, Dad, Granddad, Lily, and me—to let our scarecrow know how he performed at scaring crows away from our corn. As we go, Lily bangs the drum, *boom!-bam!-boom!-bam!* Mom plays the flute, *tu-re-lu-re-lu!* Granddad holds the ceremonial torch and paraffin can aloft. Dad waves the annual scarecrow report about like he's batting away crows only he has the eyes to see. And I follow behind my family reciting 'The Year of the Scarecrow' over and over and over, as I'm supposed to do. It was this year that Mom and Dad let me make the scarecrow, and, after making it, I named it Samuel, Samuel Scarecrow. I like the name Samuel. It's a name that plays happily in my mouth like my favourite ice cream, which is butterscotch if you want to know. If only Mom and Dad had named me Samuel instead of Thomas, Tom for short. I know another Thomas, Tom for short. He's the school bully. I hate having the same name as the school bully. I'd rather be named Samuel, like Samuel Scarecrow.

I'm scared for Samuel Scarecrow. From the scowl on Dad's face, I think he's going to read Samuel Scarecrow the worst annual scarecrow report ever. The crows ate a lot of our corn this year. And it's all my fault. I should've made Samuel Scarecrow look scarier, in the same way the other Thomas, Tom for short, looks scary. Samuel Scarecrow looks a lot like me, if I'm honest. And I'm not scary-looking, ask anyone. *Boom!-bam!-boom!-bam! Tu-re-lu-re-lu!* I don't want to see Granddad set fire to Samuel Scarecrow, which is what happens when one of our scarecrows gets a bad annual scarecrow report. If you've ever seen a scarecrow set on fire, you'd feel the same way as me. You might even cry. I always cry, I don't mind owning up to it. And when one of our scarecrows is about to be set on fire, Mom and Dad always chant: "Out of the ashes of this scarecrow will rise another scarecrow," like by saying that it will make me feel better about burning scarecrows. It doesn't. *Boom!-bam!-boom!-bam! Tu-re-lu-re-lu!* If Granddad sets fire to Samuel Scarecrow, I think I'll cry even more than when the other Thomas, Tom for short, punched one of my front teeth out, and now when I whistle it sounds like I'm haunted by ghosts, even when I whistle a sunny tune. Mom, Dad, Granddad, and Lily say I have to stick up for myself better. That's easy for them to say. They don't go to school with the other Thomas, Tom for short.

Boom!-bam!-boom!-bam! Tu-re-lu-re-lu! Here we are with Samuel Scarecrow in the bottom field. Lily stops banging the drum, Mom stops playing the flute, and I stop reciting 'The Year of the Scarecrow' over and over and over. Now, Mom, Dad, Granddad, Lily, and I circle Samuel Scarecrow, as the time has come for dad to read the annual scarecrow report. And as Dad reads, I hear that in every scarecrow category, one through ten, Samuel Scarecrow's performance numbers are as low as the number of ears of corn that came from the bottom field. Lily is already dancing a jig while playing the drum, *pa-rum-pa-pum-pum-pa-rum-pa-pum-pum!*, and shouting: "Oh boy, oh boy, a scarecrow fire!" Lily likes it when we burn the scarecrows that have failed us. I see her secretly praying all year long that we won't get any corn just so she can watch a scarecrow go up in flames, the fire laughing, *crickle-crackle-crackle-crackle*. That's my sister for you. She hates seeing scarecrows safely retire up to our house after a successful year scaring crows away from our corn for reasons she keeps to herself. "The day I have to share my bedroom with one is the day I move out," she often says.

Mom, Dad, Granddad, and Lily don't care that I made and named Samuel Scarecrow. He's just a failed scarecrow to them and there's no place in our house for a failed scarecrow. I want Samuel Scarecrow to say something, to stick up for himself, but Samuel Scarecrow says nothing; he just looks at Mom, Dad, Granddad, Lily, and me blankly, like there's no life in him at all. And didn't I give Samuel Scarecrow most of the life that was in me when I made him? I am a corn husk. His expression doesn't even change when Granddad lights the ceremonial torch so that it's hot and flaming and Mom and Dad chant: "Out of the ashes of this scarecrow will rise another scarecrow."

Somebody has to stick up for Samuel Scarecrow if Samuel Scarecrow won't stick up for himself. I don't stick up for myself when the other Thomas, Tom for short, comes after me hot and flaming, but not this time. I made and named and gave most of my life to Samuel Scarecrow. Samuel Scarecrow is me, and I am Samuel Scarecrow. I won't be Thomas, Tom for short, who won't stick up for himself. The time is here to set fire to those days! So, Mom, Dad, Granddad, and Lily—*See me sticking up for myself? Do you see?* They all see, it's what they all wanted. Dad, you said, "You're no son of mine." Mom, you said, "Why can't you be more like your father?" Granddad, you said, "I blame your Nan, may she rest in peace." And now Lily is shouting, "Oh boy, oh boy, Thomas is on fire!" while playing the drum, *pa-rum-pa-pum-pum-pa-rum-pa-pum-pum!* And Mom and Dad are yelling at Granddad for being a clumsy old fool with the ceremonial torch. And I think the *crickle-crackle-crackle-crackle* laughter of fire sounds a lot like the *crickle-crackle-crackle-crackle* laughter of crows when they're falling down blackly over our corn. What do you have to say about it, Samuel Scarecrow?

She's Jackie O'Leary

"AND EATING OUT OF BIRMINGHAM, ENG-LAND—THREE TIMES WINNER OF THE BALTI MILE, FIVE TIMES WINNER OF THE HAMPSTEAD HEATH HAMBURGER CHALLENGE, UNDEFEATED AT THE FOUR OAKS FISH 'N' CHIPS MARATHON..."

It's not exactly Premier League honours, is it? Now there's a life for you. Pity I can't kick a football for toffee. Toffee, though—I can eat a lot of toffee. A lot. More than you. More than most people. Like twenty pounds in weight of toffee. Why anyone would want to eat that much toffee is another question. But that's the life of a competitive eater for you. I eat a lot. More than you. More than most people. That's just the way it is. And when you're in my line of work, some of what you have to eat you like to eat. And some of what you eat you don't like to eat. I don't particularly care for toffee. But I ate twenty pounds in weight of it. It's what you do, when you're in my game, when you're a competitive eater. So, while I'd rather be playing for Birmingham City and scoring a goal in the last minute of stoppage time to beat Villa and win the Premier League—a girl can dream, can't she?—here I am in Paris, France, oh là là!—and how I got myself on that ferry, I'll never know. But sometimes a competitive eater has to do what a competitive eater has to do, eat what they'd never thought of eating before. And you might judge me, hate me, all you want. That's OK. I understand. You're entitled to your opinion. You can't judge me or hate me more than I judge and hate myself. So, what brings me to Paris, France? That ferry I told you about, remember? Well, that and money. A lot of money. More money than you have. More money than most people have. What else is a competitive eater supposed to do? It's not like I can quit and become a professional footballer, even if I could kick a ball for toffee. And it's not like I can quit and get a regular job, a job like you have. Those types of jobs don't pay the money I need—does your job pay you the money you need?—and I need money kind of fast. Yesterday, preferably. It's not for me, you understand. It's for April, my daughter. She's dying, you see. And there's this doctor, a French doctor, who may be able to do something about April dying. The thing is, he's pretty expensive. No, ridiculously expensive. What am I saying? He's *obscenely* expensive. You have no idea. City's new number nine didn't cost as much, which'll give you an idea of the kind of money I'm talking about. Of course, I don't have that kind of money. Are you kidding? The life of a competitive eater can pay well if you're winning, which I mostly do, but winning *all over*, not only in the UK, like at the Balti Mile, the Hampstead Heath Hamburger Challenge, and the Four Oaks Fish 'N' Chips Marathon (you heard the announcer), but at events in the US, Japan, South America, and Europe, which is a problem for me, as I've a phobia, a crippling phobia, you could say—of travelling. The shrink I went to see called it hodophobia. Fancy, huh? And not to belittle other people's phobias, but give me a fear of spiders, small spaces, clowns, any day of the week. If only that were me! I'd've competed more, eaten more, earnt more. All that money invested in the stock market, compounding interest, might've been able to pay for the French doctor's services with the click of a finger, just like that. Probably not, though. As I say, this French doctor costs the Earth. April, my precious April, is a special case. Bless her. But because I'm me, any place over the Atlantic has been a no-go zone. It's bad enough travelling within England, Scotland, and Wales as the living dead, pumped full of drug s inside of a velvet-lined coffin—for comfort and a soupçon of macabre showmanship, you understand—and then put in the back of a van and shipped to Manchester, Glasgow, London, wherever. So, yeah, trains and buses are never an option. Thank goodness! Trains and buses are driven by people I don't know, people who I can't trust to get me safely from A to B. My van, well, that's driven by my assistant, who I know and has my undying trust. His name is Igor, sorry, Guptel. Guptel doesn't like me calling him Igor, even though I call him that in the most affectionate of ways, what with him laying me to res t in my coffin. Where would I be without Guptel! I wouldn't have been on that ferry for France, that's for sure, and then in the van for Paris, that's for sure, too. I did give the customs inspector a fright whe n they opened my coffin lid in Calais and I then opened my drugged, glassy eyes. What a scream! Anyhow, it turned out Igor was right, the captain didn't steer the ferry into an iceberg, despite me reading about the ice shelves splitting and sending icebergs all over the place. Like one of those icebergs couldn't have turned up in the Atlantic Ocean to sink the ferry! So, here I am in Paris, France for this event. And Paris just happens, wouldn't you know, to be where the fancy, obscenely expensive French doctor lives, too. And it's going to go like this: I compete, I win, I take the prize money, I go and see the French doctor, and April lives beyond next week. It's got to happen. It will happen.

There's no other result acceptable. This is my last minute of stoppage time to win it all for April. Guptel asked what if I don't win, what if I lose so badly that I go back home to Birmingham in my coffin actually stone cold dead, not just put under with a cocktail of drugs enough to send a horse to Xanadu. I told Guptel to stop being so negative, that I've been training for six months, that I'm in the best eating shape of my life. But he does have a point, especially about not making it out of the ring alive. I've thought about that long and hard, believe me, but the reward outweighs the risk. What is a mother supposed to do? What is a competitive eater supposed to do? Well, they compete in an event where to the victor go the spoils so they can employ the services of a fancy, obscenely expensive Parisian doctor. And April would still have Guptel. April loves Guptel. *I* love Guptel. I wouldn't be where I am today without Guptel, on the road and off the road. He's out there in the crowd somewhere. It's nice to have him here with me. I'm not alone in this strange country, this strange city, this strange building. Back in Birmingham is April with Arthur the dog. April isn't alone either, with Arthur the dog. She's safe with Arthur the dog. She'd still have Guptel and Arthur the dog if she didn't have me. April doesn't know I'm doing this, she thinks I'm in Leicester competing, not Paris. I don't like to lie to April. But what is a competitive eater supposed to do? What is a mother supposed to do? Arthur the dog knew something was up, that I was lying. I told Arthur the dog to not let on to April that I was in Paris and not Leicester. Arthur the dog said OK, just this one time, only this one time, but you better come home. I do want to go back home, but for today I must be here. What is a mother who eats competitively supposed to do? And it's been a long journey here, more than a ferry ride. Guptel said this is what you have to do, and he showed me what I had to do for six months. Now I'm in the best shape of my life after training with Guptel. (You should've seen me chase down and get the better of that deer.) Guptel used to fight for money before he gave it up because of something he won't tell me about, it hurts too much for him to tell me. That's OK. We all live with secrets we don't tell the people we love. April doesn't know I'm here in Paris, France. And Arthur the dog won't tell, just this one time, only this time. There won't be another time, I told Arthur the dog. I said the same to Guptel for six months while he showed me how to fight. Now I can fight. Fight a lot. More than you. More than most people. And I'll need to fight a lot tonight to win. And eat of course. Eat a *lot*. More than you. More than most people. Guptel says I have to focus on my speed, agility, and nimbleness. Not only my hunger. Jackie be nimble, Jackie be quick, Jackie eat the candlestick. Yes, I ate a candle once. It was one of those avant-garde competitive eating competitions. Down in Devon it was and the candle I could just about stomach, but the rose-scented soap gave me a hard time. I won, of course, but ever since then I can't stand the smell of roses and they used to be my favourite-smelling flower. I had to dig up all my rose bushes in the back garden. Arthur the dog wasn't happy about that; he liked to smell roses. I tried to make it up to him, by replacing the roses with jasmine and honeysuckle. That didn't work out. Arthur the dog doesn't like to smell jasmine and honeysuckle; he likes to smell roses. When I go home, if I go home—I have to go home, I have to win—I'll plant another rose bush, and just the one rose bush, mind you, for Arthur the dog. It'll be my thank you to him for not telling April on me about being here in Paris, France instead of Leicester. There's somebody in the audience wearing a perfume that smells like roses. Expensive roses. There aren't many people here, but they all look obscenely expensive, like the fancy Parisian doctor. It isn't the usual crowd you see for competitive eating competitions. But like I said, this isn't your usual competitive eating competition. So here are the rules:

there aren't any rules. Anything goes. And the winner is the person, from the 13 of us, 13 from all over the world, who gains the most weight at the end of seven minutes in the ring. I weigh nine stone, four pounds, for the record. I wonder what living human flesh tastes like? Will a leg taste more gamey than an arm? Are green eyes more flavourful than blue eyes? On wolfing down a lung, will I think it tastes just like haggis? Well, I'm going to find out, because I'm going to eat as much as I can in seven minutes, while trying not to be eaten myself, of course. I bet I can eat a lot. More than you. More than everyone here in the ring with me. What's a competitive eater with a mother's instinct supposed to do? Oh yeah, for today, I'm wearing the City kit. Football boots, too. Why not? The studs might come in useful for a lunging two-footed tackle and then the kicking in of a head. It's the last minute of stoppage time, the crowd are shouting out my name, and I'm going to win it all for April. Bon appétit à moi!

"...SHE'S COMPETING OUT OF GREAT BRITAIN FOR THE FIRST TIME, SO LET'S GIVE A HUGE, WARM PARISIAN BONJOUR FOR THE ONE, THE ONLY—SHE'S THE NOS-FERATU NOSHER—SHE'S JACKIE O'LEARY!"

Hard Times in —s

Etly claps her hands and says, "The Great Scarer is coming to us! Good riddance to hard times!" Indeed, these are hard times in —s since the crows malformed across the land, from Land's End to John o' Groats. Yes, here in —s, like everywhere, our crops are pillaged. Once back in the golden years the population of —s was 987. Now it's 29. We plant, the crows come, we go hungry, and then we die. Soon we'll be out of paint for changing the population size on the —s village sign. Yes, we do like to keep things as they should be and ever were in —s, even in hard times. Today though, as Etly rightly says, there is hope for us all. Today, the Great Scarer is coming to —s, population: 29. Oh, by the way, you don't mind me not naming our village, do you? As we like to keep things as much as they should be and ever were in —s, we like our privacy, too.

So then, here we all are—the 29 of us—lining Main Street to celebrate the arrival of the Great Scarer to —s, even Alwilda who has been wheeled down in her bed. "What a day!" we all say to each other. Yes, who'd have thought the Great Scarer would choose —s for his scaring? Why, —s is but a speck on the map. Try and find us on that map if you dare. To help you, our village name is spelled: —s. We do like our privacy, remember.

"Look," Katie-Sue says, "here comes the Great Scarer now!" Katie-Sue always sees things before the rest of us, because of her eye colour. "Why, he kind of looks like Jesus, pulling that scaring cross along with him," I hear Tylor say. For that, Tylor gets a wallop about his head from his Aunt Mora. And I see Tylor look at Mora as if to s ay, *What's that for?* "He's sure to pick my field for scaring," Ashel says. "You can all go home." Ashel's claim, as I know it will, starts a war of words. "Who wants to eat rutabagas all year long?" Eveline says, who grows corn. "Oh, Eveline, you're one to talk," Millard says. "I've tasted your corn and it doesn't beat my beets." This yelling, and now the punches thrown, isn't what Edweena (the —s Welcoming Committee) had in mind for the arrival of the Great Scarer. She's got a face on her like she's bitten into a piece of Eveline's corn. Then Katie-Sue shouts, "Look, he's leaving!" She's seen before all of us the Great Scarer moving on from —s and towards —t. "Don't go!" Etly screams. "Come back to us!" Oh dear, I was afraid of this. As I said, we do like to keep things as they should be and ever were in —s. You won't tell anyone about our shameful behaviour, will you? Our privacy depends upon your silence. "Look, here come the crows!" I hear Katie-Sue shout. We'll be out of paint by the end of the day.

For Alymer

In an Erdington flat above a not-yet-open laundromat, Bob sat and waited on the edge of a single bed, his breath visible in the cold air. He was fully dressed, wearing a yellow windbreaker with the hood pulled up and tightened about his head so that all you could see were his eyes, nose, and mouth. This gave Bob the appearance of an explorer about to set off on a trek to the North Pole, but in fact he was only going to Big Marley's; though sometimes, in Birmingham, a Birmingham in the winter, it indeed felt like the North Pole up and down and across England's second city, ask any Brummie. In front of Bob was his beloved music, and not music on cassettes or CDs, it should be stated—the horror of that!—but music pressed onto vinyl: 7 inches of vinyl, 10 inches of vinyl, 12 inches of vinyl, black or coloured vinyl—yes, on vinyl, the way music was supposed to be heard, aside from going to see the band or the singer in person if they were still gigging. It was a kingdom of records! Records upon records upon records! So many years building! A towering kingdom crammed into one room, from floor to ceiling and in-between, but not, it should be said, expanding into the outlands of the miniscule bathroom he was afforded, because really there was only enough room for him in there, and besides, he didn't like the idea of his records being too close to the loo—what if they fell in when he forgot to put the seat down? This being the case, there was little space left over for personal furnishings, and so those merely amounted to a military-style camp cot for sleeping, a nightstand for his record player, and a wardrobe for his clothes. But that didn't matter. He had his kingdom of records, which was his home, his safe space, and everything was as it should be—except where was Henrietta? As usual, he'd left the window open for her daily morning visit, despite the atrocious weather. It was unlike Henrietta to stand him up.

Bob stared at the chipped saucer of milk resting on his lap. What should he do? If he waited much longer for Henrietta to climb up the fire escape and jump through the open window for her breakfast, he wouldn't be the first customer to walk through the doors of Big Marley's, and Saturday was the day for new record deliveries—records at prices he could afford even on his disastrous wage. If he didn't leave soon he'd miss out, wouldn't he? He wasn't the only vinyl enthusiast around these parts. This wasn't the way it was supposed to be. He didn't like it not being the way it was supposed to be. The way it was supposed to be was that, every Saturday morning, Henrietta would visit and lap up her breakfast milk, and then they'd catch up about what had been going on in their lives, and then Henrietta would head off on her continuing adventures, and he'd head off to Big Marley's, the first customer through the door (as always) to see what new record he could buy and bring home and listen to the rest of the day, the weekend, the next week, until he woke up to another Saturday and another record buying day and another Henrietta visit. That was his life as it should be.

Anxiety began to spread through Bob. How much longer should he wait for Henrietta? He really did want to see her. He really did want to leave for Big Marley's. What a situation! He looked at his watch.

If he left now, hurrying all the way, he'd still be the first customer through Big Marley's doors. And Big Marley would be there to greet him, regular as clockwork, if *he* was regular as clockwork, and Big Marley would say: "You should see what came in today!" Then Big Marley would laugh a Big Marley laugh, a laugh that sounded like the E string of a bass guitar being plucked, and his world couldn't be a better world. But with Henrietta missing, how could his world be a better world? Henrietta was always on time. She always visited every Saturday. Why not this Saturday? Maybe she'd found another window to jump through? Another person to visit? A person who didn't present her breakfast in a chipped saucer? A person who fed her creamier milk? Cats were fickle, weren't they? Was Henrietta fickle? She'd never seemed the fickle type, even for a cat.

The Beach Boys' angelic melodies swirled up from Bob's record player to caress him, but even the sweet-singing voices of Brian, Mike, Carl, and Al weren't enough to carry away his worries over Henrietta. Should he stay, or should he go? What would Joe Strummer do if he knew Henrietta? He'd probably say: *Go to Big Marley's. Henrietta will be back. You'll see. And she's not dead, either. I know you were gonna start thinking that. Henrietta knows how to take care of herself. She's an alley cat. A punk rock cat. So, stop worrying. Get yourself down to Big Marley's before you miss out on something special. What would your Saturday be if you didn't have something special to listen to? It would throw off your whole week. Everything wouldn't be as it should be. I'm punk rock, I could handle it. Henrietta is punk rock, she could handle it. But you're not punk rock. You may like to listen to punk rock, but you're not punk rock, I'm sorry to say. Don't be offended. Not everybody can be punk rock like Henrietta and me. Just be thankful I'm in your life. And Henrietta will be back in your life, too. Bet on it. It's all just a bit of fuzz on your stylus. Blow the fuzz away and don't stand up Big Marley. You're his*

Henrietta, you know. Do you really want to worry Big Marley the way Henrietta is worrying you? You've seen how Big Marley gets with some customers. You don't want to be one of those customers, do you?—banned for life from entering Big Marley's because you were late. Where would you go for your records?

Bob stood up as though parade ground orders had been barked into his ear, spilling a little of Henrietta's milk onto his black corduroy trousers. Now Henrietta would have less milk for her breakfast whenever she visited. It was the last of the milk, too. His breakfast had been corn flakes without milk. He'd have to do a shop on the way back from Big Marley's. He'd buy creamier milk this time. Henrietta deserved creamier milk being an alley cat, a punk rock cat. From now on, a Saturday wouldn't pass without creamier milk being available for Henrietta. How could Henrietta resist such a feast? Did he deserve creamier milk when he wasn't punk rock? He'd like to be punk rock. But que será, será, as the song went.

Time was moving on, as Joe Strummer had pointed out, and so Bob walked over to his open bedroom window, navigating tower blocks of records, taller than him, with pathways just wide enough for his slim body to slink through, cat-like. He'd encounter problems if he ever gained weight with creamier milk on his cornflakes. Only a person of his current dimensions could walk through his kingdom of records. One day, he'd have to move. It wasn't healthy for his records to be stacked atop each other, but what else was he supposed to do? When he was richer—he could dream, couldn't he?—he'd live in a big house with one whole room, or two or three whole rooms, set aside purely for his records and they'd be housed in fancy bespoke cabinetry. What a day that would be! He'd be able to find and pull out a record to play with ease, without referring to the schematic design he'd put down in his school exercise book, configurations no one would be able to decipher apart from him, with its drawings and lists and arrows and footnotes. He'd never live in a big house, build another kingdom, before he needed to buy another school exercise book. Perhaps he should buy one, along with creamier milk, on the way back from Big Marley's? He needed to be ready at a moment's notice.

At the open bedroom window, Bob looked down the fire escape zigzagging into the rain-soaked alley that separated the downstairs laundromat from the bakery that served up a delicious sausage roll opposite. He saw a metal lid suddenly lift up like a flying saucer from one of the bins pushed up against the side of the bakery, which then dropped to puddled stone with a smash and a clatter. Henrietta wasn't the cause of the disturbance, but rather the bitter and bullying wind terrorising the alley. Henrietta was nowhere to be seen. He sighed. Henrietta should be inside on such a filthy day. Him, too, for that matter. But the call of Big Marley's was too much to resist, would always be too much. The weather be damned! He placed Henrietta's chipped saucer of milk on the window sill. He'd continue to leave the window open a little. Henrietta needed a place to take refuge, if she cared to. Still, he hoped that Henrietta wouldn't again knock down part of his kingdom, one tower block of records falling into another and then into another, records falling like lined-up and pushed dominoes, while he was gone. That time, his downstairs neighbour screamed of an earthquake. Of course, he hadn't let on that it was no such thing. He'd just gone about rebuilding his kingdom with the assistance of his school exercise book, making a few modifications and improvements along the way, for which he had to gladly thank Henrietta and her curiosity at the end of the day.

"I've left your breakfast for you," Bob shouted into the alley. "Be back soon!" He then turned off the Beach Boys mid-song and left his kingdom for Big Marley's, not putting the Beach Boys record back into its sleeve and then cover, as he'd normally do, which didn't sit right with him, not at all, as there was a sleeve and cover for every record and every record should be in its sleeve and cover unless it was being played. But, yes, time was moving on. He didn't want to be late for his very important date with Big Marley. If he was punk rock, like Joe Strummer, like Henrietta, he wouldn't care about being on time, having the first pick of the records that had arrived that Saturday. Perhaps he should try working a little bit of punk rock into his life? He could be a little punk rock, couldn't he? He'd eaten corn flakes without milk for breakfast, after all. Surely that was a little bit punk rock? He'd ask Big Marley. Big Marley was punk rock, too. A whole lot of punk rock, like Joe Strummer, like Henrietta. Big Marley would know.

***

"Weetabix," Big Marley said, "Weetabix without milk would be punk rock."

"I don't like Weetabix," Bob said. "I like corn flakes. Preferably corn flakes with milk."

"You asked."

Bob sighed and looked down at the counter collaged with flyers for various gigs that had happened about the city over the years. He'd been to many of the gigs, but not all of them like Big Marley had.

"I've got a record to cheer you up," Big Marley said from behind the counter, his voice deep and resonant.

"But I have this," Bob said, handing over a record to Big Marley.

Big Marley put the record under the counter. "No Lemon Pigs today."

"I don't have it," Bob said, wanting to see the record again, take it home.

"You don't want it."

"I don't?"

"Not today. I have something better for you."

"Better?"

"Have I ever let you down before?"

"No," Bob said, which was the truth. Big Marley had never let him down. He actually liked it when Big Marley occasionally chose a record for him; it meant he didn't have to ponder over multiple records until he was sick in the mind over which record he should show commitment, which record would become part of his kingdom. On one occasion, he'd spent the whole day, from opening to closing time, in Big Marley's prevaricating over his choice of record. That time, Big Marley joked that he should've been paying him rent. At least, he thought it was a joke.

Big Marley reached back under the counter and lifted up a record for Bob to see. It wasn't the Lemon Pigs. "Straight from the US, West Virginia, the Appalachians." He handed over the record to Bob. "I thought of you immediately. It's free, too. But only free to you, my favourite customer."

"Free?" Bob held the record as though he'd just been given a new-born baby to hold, though not a Lemon Pigs baby.

"Came in on an order by mistake," Big Marley said. "And what I didn't have to pay for, you don't have to pay for."

Bob examined the old and battered album cover front and back with its golden brown colourings of skinny and dense leafy trees, with no words to say who the singer or band was, who put out the record; there were only those trees, the type of trees that somebody or something might stand behind. He held the cover to his nose and sniffed.

What was that smell? It was a smell that was familiar to him, a smell from his childhood, more prevalent than the smell of the aged record cover, a record cover a record company would never have manufactured, more a record cover that a person had crudely made from rough and thick cardboard. The four corners of the record cover weren't even right angles, they were angles that were displeasing, unsettling, to his eyes,

Big Marley smiled. "Crayons, right?"

"Have you listened?" Bob asked.

"Haven't had the time," Big Marley said. "Do you? And anyway... no, never mind."

"What?"

Big Marley looked behind him, as though expecting to see someone, something, there—and then back at Bob. "It's nothing," he said. "Trust me."

"And it's free?"

"Save yourself some money. That creamier milk will cost a bit. The new school exercise book, too. Can you afford to pass up free?"

Bob thought about the expense of the creamier milk and the school exercise book. He thought about the money in his pocket. "What about the Lemon Pigs?"

"It'll be here next Saturday."

"Will it?"

"I'm Big Marley, aren't I?"

"You're Big Marley."

"Damn right, I am," Big Marley said. "Now before you go, see that woman over there?"

Bob turned to look at the woman, around his age, give or take a year, flicking through records in the punk rock section. She'd entered Big Marley's not long after him. He'd noticed her.

"Why don't you go and speak to her?" Big Marley said.

Bob turned back to face Big Marley. "Speak to her?"

"You can speak."

"Can I?"

"You're speaking to me."

"You're different."

"Well, I'm Big Marley."

"And I'm Bob."

"Pleased to meet you, Bob. Now go and say something to her."

"Why?"

"Bob, you're killing me."

"I am?"

"What if you killed me? What if I was dead? Who'd you buy your records from? Go and speak to her. I saw you looking when she came in. See, she likes punk rock. You like punk rock. Go over there and say something. It would be punk rock."

"Punk rock?"

"Would you rather eat Weetabix without milk than talk to her?"

"Yes."

"Look, she's leaving. It's now or never."

Bob turned again to see the woman heading for the door. "I guess it wasn't meant to be."

"Go and make it be," Big Marley said, using a big hand to give Bob a big push away from the counter, towards the woman. "It'll do you the world of good. Have I ever let you down before?"

Propelled by Big Marley, Bob found himself closer to the woman than he wanted to be, both of them heading for the door. He didn't want to catch up, hugging his free record as though it were a security blanket. Should he listen to Big Marley? Speak to the woman? Big Marley had never let him down before. But what would come of it if he said something? And what should he say? What would Joe Strummer say? Joe Strummer was punk rock. What would Big Marley say? Big Marley was punk rock. He wasn't punk rock. What should he say? He wasn't cut from the same cloth as Joe Strummer and Big Marley. They were cut from denim and leather. They were punk rock, head to toe. He was cut from nylon and wool, head to toe. And he felt comfortable and safe cut from nylon and wool. He wasn't punk rock. The woman was cut from denim and leather, too. She was punk rock like Joe Strummer and Big Marley. He wouldn't say anything to the woman. He didn't have the time. There was shopping to do. He'd creamier milk and a school exercise book to buy. He didn't want the shop to run out of creamier milk and school exercise books before he got there. Henrietta would be disappointed. He'd be disappointed, if he unexpectedly ran out of room in his current school exercise book. Big Marley would be disappointed, too. Big Marley may even get angry. He didn't want to be in Big Marley's bad books. He'd seen what happened to customers who ended up in Big Marley's bad books. They were banned from Big Marley's. Where would he go to buy a new record every Saturday if he was banned for not speaking to the woman? There wasn't another record shop like Big Marley's anywhere. But Big Marley wouldn't ban him from his shop, would he? He was Big Marley's favourite customer. What was he thinking? He'd always have Big Marley's. No matter what. Yes, he'd keep on walking with his free record, past the woman, and he'd be on his way to buy creamier milk and a new school exercise book. And he wouldn't look back.

However, the best-laid plans have a way of going up in flames the very moment they're written down, and so when Bob came alongside the woman, who'd suddenly stopped on the verge of leaving Big Marley's and was now rooting through her black leather shoulder bag for something or other, it was to Bob's greatest alarm that the woman ceremoniously linked her left arm with his right arm.

The woman smiled at Bob. "Now we're engaged," she said. "You have the ring, don't you?"

Of course, Bob didn't know what to say, where to look.

"That's okay, we can pick one out together on the way to church," the woman said, hurrying Bob out of Big Marley's. "My name's Kate, by the way. What's yours?"

Bob somehow, the shock of the moment taking over him, working his mouth, gave his name.

"I always knew I'd marry a Bob," Kate said.

***

At Church Street Cafe, the sound of people's morning chatter filled the air along with the smell of frying bacon. Bob, sitting one side of a table for two, looked up from his mug of tea to see Kate still sitting across from him. She hadn't miraculously disappeared as he'd hoped, bored with his company. When would she say something? She hadn't said anything since ordering them tea for two. Perhaps she was waiting for him to say something? She'd be waiting a long time, if that was the case. Her tea would go cold. He was unused to sitting down for tea for two. Tea for one was more his cup of tea. Unlike now, he always felt comfortable sitting down for tea for one. You knew where you were with tea for one.

Kate smacked the table, startling Bob, making waves of their tea in the mugs. "You know who I adore—Dusty Springfield!" She then started singing, "You don't own me...", loud enough for every customer in the cafe to hear, to make them look over at her, eyes closed, swaying from side to side to music that only she could hear.

Bob looked at the other customers looking at Kate singing Dusty Springfield, and then they all looked at him with faces to say, *Will you shut her up? It's too early for having to cope with this kind of carry-on.* He looked back down at his mug of tea so that he didn't have to look at the people looking at him, imploring him with their faces to shut Kate up. But he'd only just met her. How was he supposed to shut her up when he'd only just met her? Someone else could shut her up. They knew her as well as he knew her. He should just get up and leave. He didn't have to be here. Right now, he should be shopping for Henrietta's creamier milk and his new school exercise book. How was he supposed to just get up and leave, though? That sounded like a punk rock thing to do. He was cut from nylon and wool, not denim and leather. But he had two feet, didn't he? Two feet that still worked as far as he knew. With two working feet, he could get up and leave. Then, as abruptly as Kate had started singing, he didn't hear her singing. He looked up from his mug of tea to see Kate drinking from her own mug of tea, as though nothing out of the ordinary had occurred, she'd been quietly drinking her mug of tea all along.

"Got any Dusty Springfield?" Kate asked.

"Yes," Bob said, immediately regretting saying so. What if Kate wanted to come back to his place and listen to Dusty Springfield records? What if she wanted to sing along to them all? His neighbours wouldn't like that, even though, he had to admit, Kate had a lovely singing voice. Not as lovely as Dusty Springfield's singing voice, but lovely to his ears all the same.

"You'll have to play me some," Kate said.

This time Bob kept quiet.

"Seeing someone, is that it?" Kate asked.

Bob shook his head.

"I'm OK, you know." Kate tapped her head, the nails on her fingers sharp and painted orange. "Up here, I mean. I just like to meet people. Sometimes the way I met you. You don't have to worry, we're not really going to get married." She giggled. "I did see you looking, though."

Bob blushed and started to crack his knuckles.

"In uncomfortable situations, I hum," Kate said. "You crack your knuckles, and I hum. Sometimes I even sing!"

Bob left his hands alone.

Kate lifted her mug of tea into the air, a toast. "Here's to nervous habits." She drank some tea. She then put the mug down onto the table, and reached over to envelop Bob's left hand inside of her right hand. "So how about it?" she asked.

***

Bob sat on the edge of his bed holding his free record from Big Marley's. He hadn't come home with creamier milk or a new school exercise book. He'd come home with Kate. Henrietta hadn't been waiting, and her milk remained untouched. He watched Kate navigate his kingdom of records, disappearing out of sight, back into sight, out of sight. She moved like a cat, slinky, secretive. She had the same dimensions as him.

"It's freezing in here," Kate said, unseen behind a stack of records, records upon records upon records.

"I'm leaving the window open for Henrietta," Bob said. It felt strange to say so much to somebody he hardly knew. He wasn't the type to say a lot to strangers. He hardly said a lot even to people he knew, like Big Marley.

"Who's Henrietta?"

"A cat."

"A friend for you. That's nice."

Bob saw a sliver of Kate appear again, looking out of the open window, down the fire escape. He heard her humming, humming another Dusty Springfield song. Then she made her way back through his kingdom, back to him, stroking, petting his records. She sat down next to him on the edge of the bed. He'd never had someone sit on the edge of his bed before. He moved over a little bit, so that his corduroy leg wasn't touching Kate's denim leg. The feeling was too much punk rock.

Kate stretched out her arms as though to embrace every last single record in the room. "All I can say is—wow!"

"The landlord says I'm a fire hazard," Bob said.

"People! What do they know? Besides, it's too cold in here to start a fire. Got any rare ones?"

"Here and there."

Kate looked about the room, up and down and across Bob's kingdom. "I read in the paper about a woman who bought a picture at a car boot sale for one pound, and then she took it to that TV show where they tell you how much your stuff is worth. And guess what? The picture turned out to be worth twenty thousand pounds! It was nothing much to look at, too. Can you believe it?" She took Bob's free record from him. "Take this record. This could pay for a vacation! A car!" She looked at the cover. "On second thoughts, though." She shivered and gave the record back to Bob. "They're the kind of trees that someone or something stands behind, if you ask me." She stood up from the bed. "Look, I really must be going."

Bob stood up from the bed, too.

They stood looking at each other.

"Want to get together tomorrow?" Kate asked.

Bob had to remind himself what day tomorrow was. The answer came to him: today was Saturday, tomorrow was Sunday, the first Sunday of the month. That meant the Lemon Pigs fan club meeting at the library. Then, afterwards, he'd come home and listen to all of his Lemon Pig records in order. If Bob Marley hadn't had his way, he would've had a new Lemon Pigs record to play: *Lemon Pigs Live at The Fox and Geese*. Instead, he'd a record with crayon trees on the cover. The kind of trees someone or something would stand behind.

"I'll take your silence as a yes," Kate said. "How about we meet at the cafe again? Nine o'clock all right with you? Now... I may be late, but wait for me. Okay? I'll buy you breakfast. Whatever you want. That bacon smelled good, didn't it? Let's have bacon sandwiches. I love bacon sandwiches. Who doesn't?" She stepped closer to Bob and kissed him on the cheek.

Bob flinched at the touch of her black-lipsticked lips.

"I can see my own way out," Kate said, humming yet another Dusty Springfield song as she went. "Tell Henrietta I said hi! She's lucky to have a friend like you, keeping the window open like that. And in this weather, too. Good grief!"

When Kate had shut the flat door behind her, gone, Bob sat back down on his bed. He cracked his knuckles. Kate hummed, hummed Dusty Springfield songs apparently, and he cracked his knuckles. What would Joe Strummer and Big Marley say about all of this? He imagined Joe Strummer and Big Marley would say: *Look at you all suddenly punk rock*. It had been a pretty punk rock Saturday morning. How would Sunday turn out? If he told Kate that he didn't like bacon sandwiches, that he'd prefer a sausage sandwich——would that be punk rock, or not punk rock? He shuddered. The bitterness inside of the flat was overwhelming. He should take off his wet clothes and put on all of his other clothes, his dry clothes, for his own health, and for Henrietta's health, too. He didn't want to close his window and have Henrietta appear thinking he wasn't home with a closed window. He'd then get into bed and maybe take a nap. Being punk rock could be tiring when he wasn't used to being punk rock. He placed his new free record from Big Marley's on top of his record player. He didn't have the ears to listen to his new free record now; they were too numb, and besides, with Henrietta missing, and the appearance of Kate, and his numb ears, for that matter, everything wasn't as it should be. He'd listen to his new free record later, when things had settled down, when everything might feel more as it should be.

***

Bob woke screaming from his nightmare. He breathed heavily, as though he'd completed a one-hundred-metre sprint, the first place prize—his life! He quickly switched on his bedside table lamp, unable to cope with the coffin darkness of his flat. The weak lamplight did little to illuminate his surroundings, little to alleviate the fear of his nightmare, unwelcomingly crossed over into his wakefulness. Within the bitter coldness of the flat, he saw each of his panting breaths, now a person of sorts, materialised wispy, raising up their hands in fright and then vanishing into hiding. He looked about his flat, his kingdom of records, once familiar to him, each record a friend—and so many friends, too, friends upon friends upon friends, friends that were now suddenly strangers, because now they didn't look like his records, his friends, at all—they were different, they didn't seem real, they were to his eyes only colourings of records, a kingdom of records coloured with crayons. He could smell the crayon.

In his nightmare, there was someone, something, standing behind a tree and then suddenly another tree, tree after tree after tree, trees coloured with crayons, golden brown crayons. He could smell the crayon. And that someone, that something, was always too fast for him to see, but he knew that someone, that something, was there—hidden behind tree after tree after tree. Except for—yes, except for, every now and again, for the briefest of moments, the blink of an eye, he'd see a pair of old and battered brown shoes, an old and battered brown hat. Then, of course, there was the giggling. He'd run, but no matter how fast he'd run, whichever direction he ran, there was no running away, there was no escape from that someone, that something, with the old and battered brown shoes, the old and battered brown hat, always closer, getting closer, giggling. He'd run into one of those crayoned trees and had fallen and had woken into strangeness. "Is that you, Henrietta?" he asked, but there came no answer, no movement, to indicate Henrietta was with him, as gradually he saw his kingdom of records begin to return to normal, become once more the friends he'd met and knew well, friends smelling like records again and not crayon. Unable to sleep, he watched and smelled this happen through the Saturday night and into a Sunday morning, when once again his kingdom of records returned to the way it was meant to be. It had only been a nightmare, the after-effects of a nightmare, it had only been a nightmare... he'd said to himself, over and over, throughout the ordeal.

***

It was the first Sunday of the month, and so Bob had met Willie at the town library meeting room—the two of them being founder members of the Lemon Pigs Fan Club, Birmingham branch, which was, to their knowledge, the only branch of the fan club in existence—and the pair of them were now sitting on red plastic chairs, which was part of a round of other red plastic chairs arranged to encourage friendly and lively discussion of all things Lemon Pigs. Bob's and Willie's bums were the only bums seated in the circle. It was the same as it ever was. There were other red plastic chairs in the room, too. They were stacked against the wall either side of the meeting room door. And this Sunday, and unlike previous first Sundays of the month, those stacked red plastic chairs made Bob feel, well... uneasy. He yawned and fiddled with a gavel resting upon a clipboard that was in turn resting on his lap. They were only stacks of red plastic chairs, red plastic chair upon red plastic chair upon red plastic chair. That's all. He shouldn't be feeling uneasy about the presence of stacked red plastic chairs. What was that all about? Didn't his uneasiness have more to do with his impending date with Kate after the meeting, at the cafe? Not stacks of red plastic chairs. Of course it did!

"Do you smell aftershave?" Willie asked Bob, sniffing the air.

"No," Bob said, sniffing the air, too. He didn't like to lie but this seemed like a moment for lying.

"Smells like Brut.'

On a whim, Bob had once bought a bottle of Brut aftershave for special occasions in his life, because, he'd said to himself, he was supposed to smell nice for special occasions. That day there hadn't been a special occasion coming up, but all the same, he'd wanted to be prepared for if and when a special occasion was announced. The bottle of Brut had also been on sale, drastically reduced in price, and so it had seemed a good buy even without the prospect of a special occasion on the horizon. Pennies saved, he'd also said to himself, meant pennies to buy a record at Big Marley's. Unfortunately, *this* day, the Brut had come out of the bottle and onto his hands quicker than he'd expected. Was this why that shipment of Brut was on sale all those years ago—faulty bottle mechanics? Being him, frugal for the sake of buying records at Big Marley's, he hadn't wanted to waste any of the aftershave and so he'd put all of it onto his face. That had been a mistake! Unused to wearing aftershave, especially that amount of aftershave, his cheeks had felt like they were being dive-bombed by hundreds of grumpy wasps. The stinging had gone away in time, a lot of time, but the smell, the strong smell of too much Brut on his face, hadn't gone away. Of course, he'd tried to wash away the smell with soap and water, but the Brut was too much competition for soap and water. Well, he couldn't let Willie know he was the one wearing Brut. Willie would ask why, and want to know about his special occasion. He'd have to lie again. What could he come up with? "Could be one of the librarians," he said.

"They're all women," Willie said.

"So?"

"Women don't wear Brut, do they?"

"Some might."

"Not these librarians."

"You don't know."

"Well, they wouldn't choose Brut." Willie sniffed the meeting room air. "Seems to be coming from over where you're sitting."

Bob cleared his throat in an officious manner, in a manner to start the first Sunday of the month Lemon Pig Fan Club meeting already, in a manner to stop the conversation about Brut aftershave and those people, female librarians included, who may or not be wearing it. "We should get started. I don't think anyone else is going to come."

"Nobody else ever comes."

"We put up flyers."

"Fat lot of good that did us."

"They were nice flyers."

"How many did you put up?"

"A hundred."

"Bloody hell. A hundred flyers and it's still just the two of us. We should both see a doctor. There's got to be something wrong with us."

"Somebody might walk through that door any second now."

"You're dreaming."

"You never know."

Bob and Willie both looked towards the meeting room door. A wall clock above the door tick, tick, ticked loud seconds passing by within the silence of the library meeting room. Nobody opened the door.

Bob and Willie looked at each other.

"There's got to be more to life on a Sunday morning than this," Willie said.

"Like what?" Bob asked.

Willie sighed. "I don't know. Just more."

"You wouldn't leave, would you?"

"That's the horror of it. I wouldn't know where to go. What to do."

Bob looked up at the wall clock above the door of the room. Time was moving on. His special occasion with Kate was approaching fast. He scratched about his chin, up around both of his cheeks. "Shall we start the meeting? I remembered to bring the gavel this time." He held up the gavel for Willie to see.

"May as well," Willie said. "Say, have you seen your face?"

"My face?"

"What's wrong with your face?"

"There's something wrong with my face?"

"From where I'm sitting."

Bob put down the gavel on his clipboard and put both of his hands to his face. It suddenly felt bumpy. And, yes, increasingly itchy. What was happening to his face?

"You look like a pizza," Willie said.

"What kind of pizza?" Bob asked.

"A pizza I wouldn't order."

"There can't be something wrong with my face. Not today."

"Tell your face that."

"What should I do?"

"Why not today?"

"What?"

"You said there can't be something wrong with your face *today*. What's so special about today?"

"Nothing."

"Is that right?"

"That's right."

"If you say so."

"I say so."

"Suit yourself."

"I will."

"Good."

"Good."

Willie huffed. "Well, with a face like that, I wouldn't go on your date."

"What date?"

"The date you're going on."

"I'm not going on any date."

"Hair brushed and parted. Wearing those shoes I've never seen you in before. The Brut you can't smell. You're going on a date."

"I don't know what you're talking about."

"You can't fool me. I know the signs of someone going on a date. I've been on dates before. Except I didn't put on Brut. Amateur mistake there, mate. Lenel for Men—that should've been your choice. Elvis wore Lenel. Lenel wouldn't have given you that face. Now there's a dating lesson from the King and me to you."

Bob banged the gavel on his clipboard. "First of all, I'd like to thank everyone for being here today—"

"Who are you talking to?" Willie asked. "Everyone is us. It's always just us."

"It's the way we start. We always start this way."

"So, you're not going to tell me? You're going to start the meeting and not tell me."

"Tell you what?"

"Who she is."

"Well, look at that—we've finished ahead of schedule for once." Bob banged his gavel on the clipboard. "Meeting adjourned." He then urgently zipped up the gavel and clipboard within his rucksack and stood up from his chair. He didn't want to end the meeting. He looked forward to the meetings, talking about the Lemon Pigs with Willie every first Sunday of the month.. But today's meeting wasn't a Lemon Pigs meeting. It had become a Bob-was-going-on-a-date meeting. Joe Strummer would've walked out, too. He was sure of that. It was the punk rock thing to do.

"You're leaving?" Willie asked.

"I've a date, if you want to know," Bob said, swinging his rucksack across his shoulder, parting the circle of red plastic chairs for his passing.

"Told you."

As Bob left, scratching his face as he went, he couldn't help again looking at the red plastic chairs stacked high either side of the library meeting room door. There was something peculiar about them, wasn't there? Then there was that smell—a smell more powerful than a quarter bottle of Brut upon his face, the smell of crayon. Yes, the red plastic chairs didn't look like real plastic chairs anymore, they looked like the colourings of red plastic chairs. He looked up and down the chairs stacked high, three stacks either side of the door, and then he saw, peeking out from the bottom of one of the stacks, the third stack, farthest to his right, a pair of old and battered brown shoes. To his utter dismay, he then saw the shoes move, ever so lightly, but move nevertheless, as though there were toes inside of the shoes, toes flexing. Was there someone, something, hiding behind the stack of chairs? Of course not. He was imagining things! This wasn't a nightmare, or the after-effects of a nightmare—this was the first Sunday of the month when everything was as it was meant to be! This too—the stack of chairs was pushed right up against the wall. It would have to be someone, something, sickly thin to be standing there, hiding; no, not even sickly thin—they'd have to be, well... it didn't bear thinking about, did it? They were just shoes, old and battered brown shoes that had been put there by a librarian, shoes a patron had forgetfully left behind, shoes waiting to be collected. Shoes didn't move of their own accord when they weren't being worn. He was being silly, absurd, yet he wouldn't look again at the shoes. Or the red plastic chairs. He wouldn't look and he wouldn't smell. He'd keep on walking with eyes straight ahead, not breathing. After all, the meeting was adjourned, and he'd a special occasion to attend, a date to go on.

As Bob opened the library meeting room door, he heard Willie shout: "Do you smell crayons?" He also heard a giggle. It didn't sound like a giggle from Willie (and besides, Willie wasn't one to express amusement of any kind) but more like a giggle from someone, some-thing, that would wear old and battered brown shoes, someone or something hiding behind a stack of plastic chairs coloured with red crayons. Was there an old and battered brown hat, too? What was he doing? Where was his mind? Such thinking would surely put him on trial for madness. Where was his mind indeed!

***

Bob knew his face was a sorry sight, but here he was nevertheless. He'd stopped to look at his reflection in the window of Pizza Takeaway on his way to Church Street Cafe. Willie had been right—his face did resemble an awful pizza. A pizza even Pizza Takeaway wouldn't sell and they sold awful pizzas. An old woman had put on a show, tutting loudly and shaking her head in disgust, moving her breakfast to another table so that she didn't have to look at him while she was eating her bacon sandwich. He should've gone home already. He shouldn't be here, sat at the same table he'd sat at with Kate previously, *their table*, with the hood of his windbreaker pulled up over his head to disguise as much of his hot and bubbly face as possible. But Joe Strummer, sporting a pizza face, would've met Kate, so he'd meet Kate, too. And so he would, too. It was the punk rock thing to do, wasn't it? Though where *was* Kate? She'd said to him that she may be late—but this late? She'd said for him to wait—but wait this long? Now, he felt part of the fixtures and fittings of the cafe, as though when closing time came, he'd be wiped down and have the lights turned off above him to darken his presence. He'd watched many people come into the cafe, order and eat their breakfasts, and then leave. He wanted to be one of those people. Though here he still was, waiting. He'd ordered and drunk three mugs of tea, tea for one three times, which he shouldn't have done, because he knew very well that drinking more than one mug of tea would give him acid indigestion, and so it had, acid indigestion to suffer through along with his inflamed face. He looked out of the cafe window onto the high street. People who lived close to him, people who he wouldn't meet and know, walked by wearing coats, hats, gloves, clothing piled upon clothing, their armour against the winter weather. Where were they all going, hunched over, their bodies old and battered by the cold and the wind and the rain, snapshots of themselves decades on, off to collect their pensions from the post office or be laid down in their coffins at the church up the road? Did they all have someone to meet as well? Their own special occasion to attend? Perhaps Kate had made dates with all of them? Perhaps that's why Kate said she may be late, was late—she was like Father Christmas, going about town for special occasions with people he would never meet and know. It was that time of year. If he was on Kate's special occasion list, he was last on that list, for sure. He'd been waiting two hours. He'd drunk three mugs of tea and had gotten acid indigestion. He hadn't eaten a sausage sandwich. Should he stay, or should he go? What would Joe Strummer say? *You should've gone already*, he'd say. *You're looking pretty desperate. And it's not a good look on top of your pizza face. It's not punk rock.* And Joe Strummer knew best, didn't he? Joe Strummer was Joe Strummer. He was punk rock. Though why was it desperate to want to meet and know someone, to meet and know someone again? At times, he was tired of seeing people he would never meet and know. He did have Big Marley and Willie and Henrietta, of course. But it would be nice to meet and know Kate more, too. That would be punk rock, even if Joe Strummer didn't think so right now.

Beyond the people struggling past the cafe window and over across the road, Bob saw bulging, black rubbish bags piled six or seven high, ready for collection outside Clara's Chippy. Was that someone, something, standing behind the black rubbish bags? *You're being foolish!*

Check your mind! Your imagination! They were wearing a hat, weren't they?—an old and battered brown hat, bobbing up and down, as though the wearer was perhaps coughing. Or what? Giggling? It was an old and battered brown hat. to accompany old and battered brown shoes. And the bulging, black rubbish bags, now he looked more closely, didn't look like real rubbish bags at all, they looked like rubbish bags coloured with black crayons.

"I can always tell the ones who are stood up. They look out of the window like you're looking out of the window, like they'll wear away the glass."

The woman's voice startled Bob. He turned to see the cafe waitress looking down at him. She'd served him three mugs of tea.

"Take it from me, love," the waitress said, "they never show. Especially after three mugs of tea. I've seen it all before. Who was it? The one you were with yesterday? Dusty Springfield?"

Bob looked back out the cafe window. The wind had blown the old and battered brown hat away. The bulging, black rubbish bags didn't look as though they were coloured with lots of black crayons anymore. Kate was nowhere to be seen.

"Nobody's worth waiting three mugs of tea for," the waitress said. "Anyway, she didn't look your type, if you ask me. And you don't look her type either. Why don't you do yourself a favour and go home? Put something on that face of yours to calm it down. A cool, damp cloth would work wonders. That and some calamine lotion. When you've been a mother, it's almost like you've been a doctor, too. Yes, that's my prescription for you. And it's as free as the NHS. Mark my words, you'll begin to look and feel like a new man, and things will return to the way they're meant to be, like today never happened." She grabbed Bob's empty tea mug. "Come on, then, let's be having you. If you don't have a home to go to, I certainly do. My feet are killing me. I can't wait to put them up and watch the tele."

Bob stood up from the table, his and Kate's table, taking with him his itching face and his acid indigestion. The chemist would be open for calamine lotion. The corner shop, too, for creamier milk and a new school exercise book.

***

With aggressively playful hands, the wind flipped the record from front cover to back cover, back cover to front cover, occasionally cartwheeling it back and forth within the alley. Bob couldn't help himself. He walked into the alley that separated the laundromat from the bakery to rescue the record. In doing so, he became a plaything for the wind, too, so much so that he felt as though he might be lifted up, up, up and away and then across town and country to be put down in a far-off place, perhaps Nottingham, his scrawny body now a tail attached to the carrier bag he was holding, now a kite, in which calamine lotion, creamier milk, and a new school exercise book clung to each other in fear. The wind was a Jumpin' Jack Flash, here, there, and everywhere, and Bob, for all of his valiant efforts, could not pry the record from its hands—until, that was, the moment the wind flung the record against the foot of the fire escape that zigzagged up the stone brick side of the laundromat, up, up and away to the window of Bob's flat. In that moment, Bob sprung for the record before the wind could capture it again and then it was his record, and literally his record, he saw—yes, he'd met and knew this record well. It was the record catalogued on page thirty-five of his school exercise book, the record usually found in Stack J, twenty records down from the top in his kingdom of records. He looked up at the window that he'd left open enough for a cat to gain entrance without ruffling whiskers or fur and he saw that it was a window now open enough for a cat burglar to gain entrance without the need for tools to jimmy open a window frame, break a pane of glass. "Come on, Dusty," he said, putting the record into his carrier bag. He then climbed the firescape while the wind called him names.

***

Bob walked about his flat as though his kingdom of records was still there for his eyes to see, for his hands to touch, the records waiting to be played—*Pick me! Pick me!* His footsteps were louder than usual in the near empty room, even though his footsteps were a mere *tip-tap*. And now, *tip-tap-tip-tap...* he would've been passing Stack M, as described on page seventy-six of his school exercise book, those records now vanished... and now, *tip-tap-tip-tap...* he would've been passing Stack F, as described on page twenty-nine of his school exercise book, those records now vanished... and now. *tip-tap-tip-tap...* he would've been passing Stack Y, as described on page ninety-seven of his school exercise book, those records now vanished... and here he was again... *tip-tap...* looking down at the chipped saucer of milk that he'd left for Henrietta on the window sill, now two boat-shaped pieces of saucer run aground in a spill of milk.

If he were to close his eyes and make a wish and then open his eyes, his kingdom of records, records upon records upon records, his friends that he'd met and had known many times, would miraculously reappear, be back home with him where they belonged. He closed his eyes and made that wish. He wished harder than all the birthday cake wishes he'd made every year as a child growing up until he was older and stopped making birthday cake wishes, as what was the point of buying a birthday cake when he was going to be alone on his birthday, and what was the point of making birthday cake wishes because they never came true. Though perhaps this wish would be granted? A wish without a birthday cake. If there was any magic in the world this wish would be granted. His wish would be heard. He wished. Then he opened his eyes, because he couldn't keep his eyes closed forever, wish forever, and instead of records coming to his eyes, all of his records that he'd brought home with him over the weeks, the months, the years, every Saturday from Big Marleys,—tears came. There was no such thing as magic in the world, and if there was, it was not meant for the likes of him.

Without his records, his flat now resembled a prison cell. He saw his bed, his bedside table, his wardrobe, and then there was his record player. He'd sold his other furniture when it became apparent that he'd need more room for more records, wanted to buy more records than his sorry job would allow, a job he didn't want to think about, not on a weekend. He'd bought eighty-seven records from the sale of his two-seater sofa. He'd almost cleared out Big Marley's bargain section. Big Marley had told him that in all his years of selling records, nobody had bought that many records in one visit from him before. He'd gotten more joy out of those eighty-seven records than he'd ever gotten out of a two-seater sofa,—it had always been a sofa for one. He wanted to sit down. He walked to his bed, again taking the path he would've taken if his kingdom of records still stood, hadn't been stolen. As he went, the phantom smell of those records accompanied his journey, swirling about his face, entering him through his nose, smells to excite the memories of the times he'd played those records—*Remember me! Remember me!* That was the smell of Sergei Prokofiev's *Lieutenant*

Kijé. And that was the smell of Manic Street Preachers' *Generation Terrorists.* There, too, was the smell of Sandra Kerr's and John F's *Music From Bagpuss.* He wanted those records back! He wanted to hear them again!

Bob slumped down onto the edge of his bed. He felt old and battered, his life all but over. There on the bed, next to him, touching his leg, was Kate's note left for him to read. If he read the note again, perhaps it would read differently? Maybe, in the shock and the horror of the situation, he'd missed reading a sentence, an important sentence, that would explain that soon his records would be returned, every one of them, as if they'd never been stolen in the first place. He wiped the tears from his eyes—he wouldn't cry anymore if he could help it, that wasn't punk rock, was it?— and read: "Dear Bob thanks for waiting for me. You're really a dear! I didn't know which record to take, so I'm taking them all. But please... NOT THIS ONE! P.S. Maybe you'll see me on Antiques Roadshow. LOL. P.P.S. No sign of Henrietta. Naughty cat. Nice meeting and knowing you—Love, your one and only Kate." No. He hadn't missed reading a sentence.

Joe Strummer would say to him: *You could call the police, but you know how I feel about them. Anyway—like the police can help. They'll just laugh at you, that's what, leaving your window open like that. Why don't you shut it already? It's freezing in here. What were you thinking—waiting so long? I told you to go. If you'd been more punk rock you would've caught her at it. Now look where you are. It's gonna take a lot to come back from this. I don't think you have it in you to start all over again. Do you? It'd be punk rock if you did.* Could he rebuild his kingdom, be punk rock? Big Marley's would be there for him, to help, just down the road, open Saturdays for him to walk through the door and be the first customer of the day. Could he really do it? But it had to be in him to do it. He'd met and known himself. He couldn't live life without records to listen to, without a record collection. Before long, a grave would be calling out to him from near ground. He needed his records like other people needed whatever one particular thing they needed to keep on going, to get up in the morning and keep on getting up in the mornings, days upon months upon years. He'd be starting from nothing, though that wasn't exactly true—was it? He looked at the Dusty Springfield record peeking out from the top of the carrier bag he'd dropped in the middle of the room. That wouldn't do. Dusty Springfield would bring back memories of Kate. He couldn't, wouldn't, allow Kate back into his life with every song that Dusty sang. He picked up the only record he could still play off the bed, where Kate had left it for him to find resting beneath her note. He looked at the front cover, the back cover, at the tall crayoned trees.

Kate had said that those were the types of trees for someone or something to stand behind. They were the crayon trees from his nightmare. Crayon trees like crayon plastic chairs. Crayon trees like crayon rubbish bags. Crayon trees and plastic chairs and rubbish bags that someone or something would stand behind wearing old and battered brown shoes and an old and battered brown hat. Someone or something for giggling. If he played the record—what would it sound like? What would he hear? Would there be singing? Would there be only instruments? What instruments? He picked up the record. He hadn't listened to a record in so long. His fingers trembled, the fingers of a person who liked to hold a beer glass but had been told they couldn't hold a beer glass, they couldn't drink, the fingers of a person who liked to hold a cigarette but had been told they couldn't hold a cigarette, they couldn't smoke. It was his only record, a record to listen to, there was no other—but what would happen on listening? His fingers reached inside of the record cover, behind the crayon trees, and then he delicately, ever so delicately, pulled out the sleeveless record inside—he'd have to correct that, he'd record sleeves to spare, every record should have a sleeve—with the fingertips of one hand. With his other hand, he set aside the record cover on his bed and then, holding the record with the palms of his hands so as not to smudge it—though he could see it was scratched, had been owned by many uncareful people before him, had been played many times before—he put the record on his record player. He watched the stylus drop onto the record and find itself within a tarnished black groove of the record, spinning around and around, the blistering, dirty white record label spinning around, too, upon which was scrawled *For Alymer* in brown crayon. Was that the name of the band?—the name for something else? The record crackled and popped and skipped, crackled and popped and skipped. There came no music, no singing, as the record continued its revolutions, crackling and popping and skipping. What had Big Marley given him? This was a record of nothing. Had Big Marley let him down? Big Marley had never let him down before. Though where was the music, the singing? He needed to listen to music, song—any music, any song! It had been so long, so very, very, long.

It was then that Bob saw Henrietta appear at his open window with an *I'm here!* miaow. His heart palpitated with a little joy. He watched Henrietta settle herself on the window sill and look down at her once chipped saucer, now a broken-in-two saucer, at her spilled milk. He'd make it up to her with a saucer that was his best saucer, with creamier milk. Though why Henrietta looked like a cat coloured with orange and yellow crayons, he didn't know. But that was only his imagination playing tricks on him again, nothing but another unsettling fancy, it had been quite the weekend, after all, so was it any wonder he was perpetually seeing things? Whatever, Henrietta unquestionably fitted right in and was at home within his flat, now being coloured in with black and grey crayons. More wicked imagination! He wouldn't succumb to it! Where was his music? Where was his song? He heard nothing, only crackles and pops and skips. If he'd his Lemon Pigs records, the Lemon Pigs record that Big Marley had taken away from him—he'd be all right! When he listened to the Lemon Pigs everything was all right, things were put back as they should be when they *weren't* as they should be. The way things were meant to be! There wouldn't be, for instance, as when things weren't as they should be, someone, something, wearing an old and battered brown hat and old and battered brown shoes stepping out from behind the wardrobe, stepping out to music and song, old and battered music and song, now coming from the record playing, a record upon which other records would rise to build him a brand new kingdom—a kingdom of records bigger and better than before! He wanted to meet and know those records, but before that he'd have to meet and know the someone, the something, wearing the old and battered brown shoes and the old and battered brown hat. They weren't for being ignored, giggling as they were. Most foul and wicked imagination!

Painted Tin Soldiers

W hat happens now, I don't know. Auntie Fern was waiting for me at my door when I got home from school. My door is number 78. "You're having tea with me tonight," Auntie Fern said. "Your mom and dad are having a talk." Then Auntie Fern took me two doors down to hers at number 82 and unlocked the painted tin soldiers for me to play with before tea. Mom and Dad weren't having a talk. They were fighting. I could hear them behind my door. I've got dog ears.

Mom and Dad fight all the time. I'm in the middle of them at number 78. I've lined up the painted tin soldiers so they're facing each other, red-painted tin soldiers on the left and blue-painted tin soldiers on the right. The painted tin soldiers belong to Auntie Fern's Robin, that's her son, who left Auntie Fern because he's grown up. Auntie Fern usually locks the painted tin soldiers in the glass cabinet in the corner of her living room. "My Robin painted all of them himself," Auntie Fern said when she gave me the painted tin soldiers, but I knew that already. Auntie Fern just likes to say those words. I think it helps her remember when Robin was with her at number 82 and she'd make him stew and dumplings for tea. Auntie Fern is making stew and dumplings for my tea now. The painted tin soldiers are pretty. Why can't I have a school uniform like the painted tin soldiers' uniforms? I'll ask Robin to paint my school uniform from grey to red or blue when he comes back to number 82 for Auntie Fern to make him stew and dumplings for tea.

Auntie Fern isn't my real auntie. Dad told me she's just Mom's friend who lives two doors down at number 82. I like Auntie Fern, even if she's not my real auntie. She makes me stew and dumplings and she lets me play with the painted tin soldiers. And her maisonette is nice and peaceful. That's because she has nobody to fight. All she has at number 82 are the painted tin soldiers that live behind glass since Robin grew up and went away. But now the painted tin soldiers are out from behind the glass and down on the green carpet with me, red-painted tin soldiers on the left and blue-painted tin soldiers on the right. I'm in the middle of them. The painted tin soldiers tell me they want to fight. They've been behind glass for a long time, they say. That's what soldiers do: they fight. Like moms and dads. I won't tell Auntie Fern that the painted tin soldiers said they want to fight. Auntie Fern told me to play nice and peacefully with the painted tin soldiers. I think she meant by that: no fighting. Auntie Fern's in the kitchen making stew and dumplings for my tea. The less she knows about what the painted tin soldiers want to do, the better off she'll be, I think. That's what Auntie Fern said to me when she took my hand and brought me to hers at number 82. She told me, "The less you know, the better off you'll be." She'd a face like a scrunched-up crisp packet when she said those words. I didn't say to Auntie Fern that I know a lot already. You can't help it when you're in the middle of my Mom and Dad two doors up at number 78. Anyway, I've got dog ears.

The red-painted tin soldiers on the left and the blue-painted tin soldiers on the right look at each other, wanting to fight. I'm in the middle of them, and what happens now, maybe I know. "How are you doing in there?" Auntie Fern asks from the kitchen. "Okay," I say. I don't tell her that the red-painted soldiers have fired their first bullets and the blue-painted soldiers are firing back. Can Auntie Fern hear the painted tin soldiers firing their muskets? She hasn't got dog ears like me. Once, I called the painted tin soldiers' muskets 'guns.' But then Auntie Fern said the guns were called muskets, and the knives attached to the end of the muskets weren't knives, like I'd called them, they were bayonets. Auntie Fern also told me that the red-painted tin soldiers were British and the blue-painted tin soldiers were French. At school, I'm learning French, so I understand a little of what the blue-painted tin soldiers are saying, like « fue » which means "fire," and « aller » which means "go." I also know the French word « maisonette » which means 'little house,' because Mom and Dad and I live in one, two doors up at number 78, and so does Auntie Fern, right here two doors down at number 82. I understand all of what the red-painted soldiers are saying, because they're British like me.

There are red-painted tin soldiers on the left and blue-painted tin soldiers on the right, fallen down dead on the green carpet. There's smoke in the air from the soldier's muskets, but that could be from the kitchen, because Auntie Fern says, "I'm browning the stew meat. The butcher always gives me such lovely cuts of stew meat. A good price, too. I think he fancies me. But I don't fancy him." I can't see the browning stew meat, but it smells good. I'm in the middle of the red-painted tin soldiers on the left and the blue-painted tin soldiers on the right, watching them fight and fall down dead. That's what soldiers do: they fight and they fall down dead. Mom and Dad never fall down dead when they fight, but sometimes I wish they would fall down dead like the painted tin soldiers do. I'm a bad person to think like that, I know I am, but I think it all the same. I can't help it. « Aidez-moi ! » a blue-painted tin soldier says, which means the same as the red-painted tin soldier saying, "Help me!" I don't think Auntie Fern can hear the painted tin soldiers asking for help over her banging pots and pans in the kitchen. *Kerchutt-pooofff!* the musket says. "Help me!" the red-painted tin soldier on the left says. *Kerchutt-pooofff!* says the musket. « Aidez-moi ! » the blue-painted tin soldier on the right says.

I've got dog ears, even two doors down from number 78 at number 82. *"Get out, I hate you! Look what you've done! I can't go on like this! Get out and don't come back, or I'll kill you next time! Do you hear me? I'll kill you!"* "Help me," I say when I'm in the middle of Mom and Dad fighting at number 78. But no one ever hears me. No one ever helps me. So why should I listen to the painted tin soldiers or help them when they say, "Help me!" and « Aidez-moi ! » here at number 82? The painted tin soldiers asked to fight each other. That's what soldiers do: they fight and they fall down dead. It serves them right for fighting. If Mom and Dad fall down dead, it would serve them right, too. I shouldn't think like that, but I do. It's got so I can't help thinking it when nobody ever helps me stop thinking it.

"Are you sure you want dumplings with your stew?" Auntie Fern asks from the kitchen. Auntie Fern makes the best stew and the best dumplings. "Only joking," she then says. "Dumplings coming up." I always say yes to dumpling with my stew when Auntie Fern brings me two doors down to number 82 for my tea. But she's never let me play with the painted tin soldiers before. She's being nice because of the way Mom and Dad were fighting two doors up at number 78. *"No, you get out and don't come back! I'm sick and tired of looking at you day in and day out!"* Mom says. *"Kill me? No, you get out before I kill you!"* Dad says. I've got dog ears. Who'll win the war two doors up at number 78? Who'll win the war two doors down at number 82? It seems to me that everybody has to fall down dead before everything is ever nice and peaceful.

Auntie Fern's talking to someone on the phone in the kitchen. She doesn't want me to hear, because she's kind of whispering rather than talking normally, but I've got dog ears. Dogs can hear things four times farther away than humans can hear things. I learned that in my *1001 Things to Know* book I got for my birthday. I also got to know about a 1002nd thing, too. Learning about a dog's hearing was the 18th thing. We can't have a dog two doors up at number 78. It's not allowed. People are allowed, and from what I've seen at home, it's Mom and Dad that shouldn't be allowed. Not a dog. Auntie Fern doesn't know I can hear like a dog. Mom and Dad don't know I can hear like a dog either. Dad shouts: *"I don't want to do this again! Won't you ever stop! I don't feel well! I have a lot to do, and I don't feel well! And you won't stop! Please stop!"* Mom shouts: *"You think I want to do this? It's not what I want, you know. But here we go again! And look at me! Do I look well? I wish it would all stop, too! Won't it ever stop!"* Then there is Auntie Fern on the phone: "They're at it again. Only worse. You should've heard them. They had me take him, poor bugger. I'm making his tea now. It's not the first time. But what can I do? I'm in the middle." Auntie Fern can't help being in the middle, like me.

I really don't want to hear mom and dad fight two doors up at number 78, but I've got dog ears and when you've got dog ears you can't help hearing two doors down at number 82. *"We're going to lose everything! How could you do it? I trusted you! No! Don't you come near me! I'll do it, I swear! I'll kill you!"* Mom shouts. *"I trusted you, too! And where were you? How could you do it? It's me who should kill you, I swear!"* Dad shouts. I'm still in the middle wherever I am with my dog ears. But I read about how not to be in the middle in *1001 Things to Know*. It was the 1002nd thing to know. When I read it, I didn't believe it. There shouldn't have been a 1002nd thing to know in a book of 1001 things to know. I don't think I should know about the 1002nd thing, but it's in the book, so it must be allowed for me to know about it, or it wouldn't be in the book. Auntie Fern doesn't know I know the 1002nd thing. She's in the kitchen making stew and dumplings for my tea here at number 82. Mom and Dad don't know I know the 1002nd thing. They're two doors up at number 78 with their fighting. I'm here with the painted tin soldiers, and I know the 1002nd thing. *Kerchutt-pooofff! Kerchutt-pooofff!* The painted tin soldiers wanted to fight, so I let them fight. I know a 1002nd thing.

"Look, I've got to go," Auntie Fern says on the phone from inside the kitchen. "His tea's ready." I've dog ears. Auntie Fern's green carpet once looked like a pretty field of red and blue flowers. Now all the flowers are cut down except for two flowers still standing: one red-painted tin soldier on the left and one blue-painted tin soldier on the right. The red-painted tin soldier and the blue-painted soldier still want to fight and fall down dead. It's like they can't see all the other flowers cut down. Mom was wearing red when I went to school and she was on the left, and Dad was wearing blue and he was on the right. It was like they couldn't see me. "Time to pack up," Auntie Fern says from the kitchen. "Tea's ready." She means pack up the painted tin soldiers. But there are still two painted tin soldiers who want to fight and fall down dead. Mom and dad bought me *1001 Things to Know* and they wouldn't have bought me the book for my birthday if they didn't want me to know the 1002nd thing to know that's in the book of 1001 things to know.

The woman at number 80, her name is Katerina, is in the middle of number 82 and number 78, and she's talking to people who have walkie-talkies and the walkie-talkies crackle and pop like Rice Krispies crackle and pop. I've got dog ears. What happens now, I hope I know. Katerina at number 80 grows flowers outside of her maisonette and the flowers are called daphne. Katerina is from Greece. Not Britain, or France. Katerina taught me how to say good morning to the flowers in Greek, and that's "kaliméra daphne," and good night to the flowers in Greek, and that's "kalinichta daphne." Sometimes, when Katerina isn't looking, I pop the daphne like balloons. Sometimes it's something to do. I shouldn't do it, they're pretty red and blue flowers. They're not grey, like my uniform that Robin will paint red or blue for me one day when he comes back to number 82 for Auntie Fern to make him stew and dumplings for tea. *"He's probably next door at number 82. He always goes there when they're at it,"* Katerina says. *"Sounded like guns going off, it did. Are they okay?"* I've got dog ears and know a 1002nd thing that nobody else knows.

I don't need dog ears to hear the doorbell ring here at number 82. Neither does Auntie Fern bring me my stew and dumplings. "Here's your tea, Robin." Auntie Ferns says. "Oh, look—you didn't pack your painted tin soldiers away." I like Auntie Fern even though she got my name wrong, and has a scrunched-up crisp packet face when she goes to answer her door, number 82, two doors down from number 78. "You eat your tea now, before it gets cold," Auntie Fern says as she goes to answer the door. "I'll send whoever it is away so it's nice and peaceful for your tea." What happens now, I know.

Back at the Old House

These dark wretched streets going on and on and on, I can't, I can't, I can't go on anymore. Then why am I running in my new stupid shoes when I want them to take me, I want them to have me? For it to be a game? They can catch me if they can! And to be theirs—wrapped up in cold tough embraces! No longer alone back at the old house! (*Oh, all the lies you tell yourself!*) So, stop running, you'll throw up over your new stupid shoes, you know.I shouldn't have drunk so much, eaten so much, gone out so much. I should've stayed at home, back at the old house. But I'm allowed a Friday night, aren't I? Just the once—*the once!* I don't want to be back at the old house on a Friday night. Alone. (*Oh, all the lies you tell yourself!*) They'll fall all over me when they catch up, and what will they do then? Maybe they'll... will they? I shouldn't have said what I said to them, but I said it, I couldn't help myself, and they couldn't help themselves coming after me in my new stupid shoes, a pack of wild dogs. But I couldn't have gone out on a Friday night in my old shoes. People would've looked and pointed at me. *Look at him*, they would've said, *ruining our*

Friday night with those old shoes! I'm allowed a new pair of shoes, aren't I? No, I'm not. When the bills and the rent are late, I shouldn't have bought a pair of new stupid shoes—the cheapest in all of Manchester! And not in my size! Where are they—those handsome hooligans? Catch me throwing up if you can! Here I am, out of commission, yours for the taking, the having. I'm here, not alone back at the old house. (*Oh, all the lies you tell yourself!*) She gave me extra chips and gravy. (*Oh, all the lies you tell yourself!*) She didn't give you extra chips and gravy. She smiled the prettiest smile at me. (*Oh, all the lies you tell yourself!*) She didn't smile at you. Will I make the news? There were three of them, maybe four, standing there in the shadows waiting to make the news. What a relief it will be when they catch up. This is death enough! Yes, here I am, out of the shadows, waiting for you in my stupid new shoes covered with extra chips and gravy. The cheapest shoes were the most expensive shoes I could buy. If I went back, what would I say to her other than ask for chips and gravy? What if she didn't give me extra chips and gravy again? (*Oh, all the lies you tell yourself!*) She didn't give you extra chips and gravy. What if I smiled and she didn't smile the prettiest smile back? (*Oh, all the lies you tell yourself!*) She never smiled at you. Where are they? Why were you running? *Please*, I don't want to be alone back at the old house. (*Oh, all the lies you tell yourself!*) I can't go on in these new stupid shoes. They may make the news. The reporter will ask an eye-witness: *How did you feel when you saw the shoes?* And the eye-witness will say: *There they were—a pair of shoes! Without a person in them! And god knows what was on them! It threw a spanner in the works, I'll tell you. I got to thinking of things I didn't want to think about, not at my age. And I fought in the war!* They didn't catch up. They should've caught up with me in my new stupid shoes. Did they even try? How pitiful you are that *even they* didn't want you! And I'll be back at the old house soon, and those that I sometimes see there, unearthly, out of the corner of my eye, those that I sometimes hear there, whispering that one night they'll take me, have me, can finally, this night, take me, have me. I won't be alone. Not anymore. *My name is Sheryl*, she said. She smiled the prettiest smile at me and gave me extra chips and gravy. (*Oh, all the lies you tell yourself! Oh, all the lies you tell yourself! Oh, all the lies you tell yourself!*)

Sacrifices

Mom and Dad said I have to do better at learning to do without, which means I'm not their cute little girl anymore. We've fallen awful poor and have to make a whole lot of sacrifices and that means selling a whole lot of what we have to get the money to give to the big bad trouble that will knock at our door, which I think will be like when the big bad wolf visited the three little pigs in one of my reading books. Mom and Dad said we can't be blind to our downfall and we have to have our eyes wide open to see what needs to be done to break free of our devil's holding before it's too late for all of us. Two of the little pigs were blind to their downfall, and the big bad wolf ate them all up. *Oinkkkkk!* Mom and Dad built our house out of wood, and sticks are wood, and the big bad wolf ate the little pig that lived in the house that was made of sticks. Why Mom and Dad didn't build our house out of bricks, I don't know. At least they didn't build our house out of straw, so that's something I guess.

I don't want the big bad trouble to come visiting and blow our stick house down and eat Mom, Dad, and me because of our downfall. That's why Mom and Dad put me outside of our stick house with Nan and all the sacrifices that used to be inside of our stick house. Mom and Dad stuck yellow rounds on all the sacrifices we have to sell to get the money to give to the big bad trouble, and all the yellow rounds have prices written on them in black marker, like they price everything at Gem's Market, which we used to visit every Saturday for what we needed before we had to learn to do without. I miss Mr. Kipling's cakes, and I talk a lot about missing Mr. Kipling's cakes when I shouldn't, which I guess is one reason I'm not Mom's and Dad's cute little girl anymore.

The sacrifice I'm sitting on now has a yellow round stuck to it that says fifty pounds, which was the sacrifice Nan was sitting on before the long black car came. I'd been sitting on the sacrifice with the yellow round stuck to it that says five pounds, which was like sitting on a bag of rocks. This sacrifice, the fifty-pound one, is like sitting on the soft moss down by the stream, where I like to secretly go and watch the water come from wherever it's coming and go to wherever it's going. It's ever so nice to secretly watch Nan in the back of the long black car go to wherever she's going, as well. Nan was the real devil holding on to us, if you ask me, taking up space and doing nothing but making things hard for Mom and Dad and me. Nan couldn't even make a Yorkshire Pudding rise, and what's the point of a Nan if they can't make a Yorkshire Pudding rise? But Mom and Dad never asked me about what I thought of Nan, because I'm little like a little pig. *Oinkkkkk!* If Mom and Dad had asked me about Nan, I'd have told them that she was the devil they spoke about, come to live with us after she drove the tractor and knocked Granddad down to never get back up again. Don't think I don't have my suspicions about that, because I do.

Mom had been right that no one would come and buy any of our sacrifices without putting an advert in the paper, and Dad had been right that a sign at the side of the road would work just as well as an advert in the paper for fishing in the special sort of buyer we were after and doing that wouldn't cost a penny. Mom was right because nobody had come all day long and bought any of our sacrifices. Dad was right because finally a special sort of buyer came and bought Nan and took her away in the long black car. *Oinkkkkk!*

Nan hadn't liked the look of the long black car driving up to our stick house because, she said, it gave her the fidgets, as did the man and the two little pigs inside it, because they looked like they weren't from around our parts. Nan said she'd never had a pleasant encounter with someone who wasn't from around our parts in any of the eighty-six years God had looked after her through thick and thin.

I suppose Nan has a good ear for hearing alarm bells, because the man had gotten out of the long black car with the two little pigs and soon enough pointed at Nan and asked me if she was for sale. That made the man the special sort of buyer Dad was fishing for with his road sign that didn't cost us a penny. I caught on quickly. The man said that his two little pigs needed a new nan because something had happened to their old nan. The man didn't say what had happened, but I heard the two little pigs go *oinkkkkk!* when he said that about their nan and then the two of them stuck to my nan like flies on a cream bun, so sticky she couldn't swat them away with her hands for all of her trying.

I did think about what the man was asking for a long minute, because I wanted it to seem like Nan was precious to me and selling her was something I could only do for a number that was taller than the oak trees crowding around us and listening in. When I'd done all the acting my face could manage, I told the man I could sell Nan to him for the tallest number I could think of, taller than the oak trees even, and the man said that it was a number he'd be willing to accommodate. And if Mom and Dad had a taller number in mind, they should have put a yellow round on Nan, that's what I say.

I never saw Nan kick up such a stink before and she'd kicked stinks up larger than the dog that ran off with baby Emma in its mouth two springs ago. I tried to calm Nan down by telling her that she could be as much a sacrifice as Mom's sewing machine or Dad's box of tools or my reading books and that she should be happy that being a sacrifice meant the big bad wolf that was coming to our stick house would have to go hungry. Nan didn't like to hear me say that. *Oinkkkkk!*

Mom and Dad will be surprised when they come back from seeing Uncle Billy for the money they had lent him and never gotten back. Dad said it was likely a waste of time going, but it would be hard telling not knowing if they could get the money from Uncle Billy if they didn't drive all the way to his place and give it a try. Now it won't matter if Mom and Dad didn't get the money from Uncle Billy and that the sacrifices with the yellow rounds on them didn't sell. Now we have money that's taller than the tallest oak tree to give to the big bad trouble. Mom and dad said I had to do better at learning to do without, and if I can learn to do without Nan, Mom and Dad can learn to do without Nan, too.

And look, here come Mom and Dad driving up to our stick house now. They look years older, like strangers. How can that be? Never mind, their faces will change back to the faces I know when I tell them how I wasn't blind to our downfall and had kept my eyes wide open to see what needed to be done to break free of our devil's holding before it was too late for all of us. Mom and Dad will happily lift me up like they used to, and say I'm their cute little girl again.

Oinkkkkkkkkkk!

Ottilie's Obituary

Wilfred hopped out of bed, a child again at eighty-seven. What a Saturday this would be! He'd thought about this day all week long, since Ottilie's cremation the previous Saturday. Yes, even in death, dearly-departed Ottilie had managed to ruin one of his Saturdays. Of course, he'd tried his best to arrange the cremation for the Monday afterwards—not the Sunday, as he liked a lie-in on a Sunday—but those at the crematorium were having none of it. It was their busiest time of the year for deaths and if he didn't want them to do their job, he'd have to take Ottilie back home with him—it was a Saturday cremation or nothing, take it or leave it. Ottilie had still come home with him, nevertheless. It was another arrangement made on Ottilie's part, an arrangement unbeknownst to him, in order to make his life difficult, as in life, as in death, he was sure of it. She'd been clever enough. For as some were scared of spiders or knives or public speaking, Ottilie had always been scared of fire in all of its appearances: coming up out of the gas cooker, his cigarette lighter, the leaf bin at the end of the garden. So, why had Ottilie suddenly made it known to Gertrude, her sister, that she wanted a cremation rather than a burial? To continue making his life a misery—that's why! She'd known that if she'd been buried up at the church, he'd never have gone to visit, lay down flowers, say a few words. But cremation!—Well, she'd truly be able to remain in his life, cosy in her urn. She'd been clever enough all right. She knew that there was no room left in the crematorium's columbarium. Of course, too, he'd spoken to those at the crematorium about disposing of Ottilie, but they again were having none of it. Ottilie was his problem. And that was Ottilie for you—always a problem! A problem for sixty years! She'd known he'd be unable to get rid of her in her cremated state. Clever, clever Ottilie. All week long, since the Saturday cremation, he'd tried to dispose of Ottilie and had failed miserably. He'd attempted to dump her off a bridge into the river beneath and he'd brought her back in to the house; he'd driven out into the middle of nowhere to leave her in a field and he'd brought her back in to the house; he'd put her outside on the street for the bin men, and he'd brought her back in to the house. Each time, he couldn't help thinking: What if Ottilie didn't like what he'd done, and returned to the house to haunt him! He wouldn't put it past her. Clever as a fox, was Ottilie. But this was a new day, a new Saturday, a new beginning! It wasn't as though Ottilie was flesh and bone inside of the house, was it? She was only inside of an urn, all ashes, resting quiet and harmless. How could she possibly ruin this Saturday, this most joyous of Saturdays, as she'd ruined countless Saturdays before? Yes, what a Saturday this would be! Starting with a fry-up!

Wilfred placed his plate of two fried eggs, three rashers of streaky bacon, two pork sausages, baked beans, black pudding, and two rounds of fried bread onto the kitchen table, next to a mashing pot of tea. What a sight! His stomach rumbled. He couldn't wait to tuck in to all of his favourites. This was the way to begin a Saturday, and no mistake! There was only one thing missing—the Saturday morning paper. As if on cue, he heard that day's news being stuffed through the letterbox. "Right on schedule," he said to himself, walking out of the kitchen and into the hallway to collect the newspaper that was now lying on the carpet, waiting to be picked up and read. The Saturday morning paper was the best newspaper of the week with the back pages, from top to bottom, full of Saturday football to read about, and there were sure to be pages and pages about Villa's match against City later: a match, this Saturday—what a truly joyous Saturday it was!—he was going to see rather than watch on the tele. There he'd be in the Holte End cheering Villa on to victory. What a Saturday! Oh, what a Saturday! And gone, finally gone, may she rest in peace without another word uttered, was Ottilie to stop him from going to the match. No longer would the little money that came into the house have to be put towards other things instead of buying a ticket to watch Villa play at home. No longer would he have to drive Ottilie every Saturday to see Gertrude, may she rest in peace without another word uttered, too. This joyous Saturday, he'd eat his fry-up and drink two mugs of tea while reading all about how Villa were going to put three past City, and then he'd go to watch Villa do exactly that, cheering them on all the way. Now that's what he called a Saturday! A Saturday to remember! A Saturday to kick off a whole new calendar of Saturdays, the way Saturdays were supposed to be enjoyed!

Wilfred bent over to pick up the Saturday morning paper and heard a new spot of moaning within his back joining the chorus of another hundred or so spots of moaning coming from his back. It wasn't any fun getting older and older and older; there was always a new bodily discomfort to wake up to, making itself known. On the brighter side, though, there was no Ottilie about the house reminding him of his Saturday chores. A laundry list of Saturday chores. So, all things considered, he could put up with his brittle back. Ottilie never had back pain; in fact, she'd never talked about the pain of old age at all. She'd gone ahead and died as if she were fit as a fiddle, with the body of a young striker in top form knocking in goals from all over the pitch. That had been annoying. He'd put a stop to that. Ah, Ottilie's garden! It had been her life. Little had she known that it would bring her life to an end. That, and her love of Agatha Christie novels. She loved those novels as much as he loved reading the Saturday morning paper sports pages. He'd read *one* of the novels, though—just the one, for research purposes—the one Ottilie had mentioned because there was foxglove, the murder weapon of choice in the story, growing in her garden, too. "Lovely, deadly foxglove," Ottilie had said. And lovely and deadly it had been! No one had ever suspected a thing. It was just her time to go, they'd all said. Eighty-five was a good innings. They'd never read Agatha Christie, apparently. They didn't know about foxglove. He chuckled. It wasn't only Ottilie who could be clever. He took his morning paper back to the kitchen, experiencing a new moaning in his right foot joining the chorus of another hundred or so spots of moaning coming from his right foot. He wondered when his left foot would catch up and give him more bother, too. It always did.

Wilfred sat down at the kitchen table to enjoy his breakfast. He smiled. There was nothing you couldn't do starting a Saturday with a fry-up, a pot of tea, and the morning paper. You could conquer the world if you were that way inclined. You could do all the things you'd dreamed of doing, but had never gotten around to doing because you hadn't started a Saturday with a fry-up, a pot of tea, and the morning paper. Previously, his Saturday mornings had been taken up driving Ottilie to see Gertrude, who lived in Coventry and, according to Gertrude, was dying in Coventry, too. Going to see Ottilie's sister every blessed Saturday meant there was never time for a fry-up, a pot of tea, and the morning paper. Gertrude had been dying for as long as he could remember, dying of this or that or something or the other. She was a receptacle for all the life-threatening ailments known to medicine. And some unknown, too. She'd attended Ottilie's funeral, right as rain, looking like she'd outlive everyone in attendance. "When it's my time, and that might be tomorrow," Gertrude had said, "I hope I have such lovely flowers everywhere." He'd picked, and arranged, the flowers for the funeral from Ottilie's garden. He wasn't going to the expense of paying the florist down the road when he had his choice of free flowers growing in the back garden. That money had been earmarked for the ticket to watch Villa play City later. Of course, he hadn't picked foxglove. Some flowers were best kept in the garden. A lovely, deadly secret. Now he'd never have to drive to Coventry and see Gertrude on a Saturday again. She'd had the nerve to call him on Wednesday. "Are you still coming up? I won't be around for long, you know," Gertrude had said. He'd told her that he wasn't coming up and he wouldn't ever be coming up again and then he'd hung up the phone. He'd felt good telling Gertrude what was what. He was living a new life now, an about-time life, and car trips to see people he didn't want to see and had never wanted to see weren't on his itinerary.

What *was* on his itinerary, right now, was his breakfast. He knew what Ottilie would've said to him about his breakfast plate. "You can't eat that," she would've said. "Not at your age. You've got to think of yourself, and you've got to think of me. What would I do if you were to die before me?" He had thought of Ottilie, and he'd thought of the Agatha Christie book, and he'd thought of the foxglove—just enough foxglove in Ottilie's tea at the breakfast table. She was always drinking flowery teas. He couldn't stand the smell or taste of them. He was a PG Tips man, and he'd be a PG Tips man to the day he died. Funny how a flowery tea can kill you off quicker than a plate of two fried eggs, three rashers of streaky bacon, two pork sausages, baked beans, black pudding, and two rounds of fried bread. "Isn't that right, Ottilie?" he asked, looking at Ottilie's urn sitting right next to the teapot on the kitchen table. "Nothing to say? Well, I don't blame you, given your condition." Call it whimsy, but he'd the splendid idea the day before of sharing his breakfast with Ottilie one last time, for old time's sake. Then, he would put her somewhere out of sight and out of mind, maybe in the cupboard under the stairs with the suitcases and the spiders. That would work out handsomely.

Wilfred tucked into his breakfast with gusto. What a breakfast! What a Saturday! "Now for the paper," he said. He put down his knife, while still using his fork to shovel black pudding into his mouth, and flipped the paper over from the front page to the back page. He wanted to read all about the Villa match. Instead, he saw a large black and white photo of Ottilie. Ottilie, his dead wife. Ottilie inside of the urn on the kitchen table next to the pot of tea. The shock was enough to make the black pudding tumble from out of his mouth, to make him drop his fork to the kitchen floor, to make him jump up from his chair and skedaddle over to a corner of the kitchen where he clung to the cooker for emotional support. What had he just seen? That really wasn't a photo of Ottilie on the back page of the paper, was it? He'd only imagined it. His eyes were playing silly buggers. He was used to his back acting up, but it was the first time for his eyes. He'd always had good vision; it was the one of the parts of his body, even in his ripe old age, that hadn't cascaded into feebleness. He was glad of that, as he didn't have the face for wearing glasses. He'd the face for a hat—his trilby—but not glasses. Old age, like Ottilie—always out to spoil a Saturday! He didn't want to go to the optician about his eyes. It was bad enough going to the doctor when his back and feet were acting up. The optician wouldn't have a pair of glasses that sat well on his face. As for contact lenses, no thank you very much. What if they shifted and ended up inside of his head? Of all the days of the week for his eyes to suddenly go for a burton—the Saturday he was going to watch

Villa beat City. What if he saw Ottilie out on the pitch, one of the Villa players? He'd just seen her on the back page of the paper; she could show up playing midfield for Villa, too.

Wilfred put a hand to heart, to usher it back where it should be, not madly beating at his ribcage to be let out. Surely he was only getting away with himself. It had been a stressful week with Ottilie's funeral, not to mention the flower arranging and attempting to offload Ottilie's ashes. Was it any wonder he was now seeing things? Such events would be enough to make a younger man, a younger man with twenty-twenty vision, go doolally in the eyes. Really, it was a photo of a Villa player on the back page of the newspaper, and not Ottilie. His eyes were all right. His eyes had always been all right. And he'd go to the grave with his eyes being all right. He should write it down that when his time came he wanted to donate his eyes to the medical profession for them to be studied and written about in distinguished journals with the conclusion being that it was a wonder of human existence that he, Wilfred Rossiter, had reached a hundred with eyes that were still all right. That wasn't Ottilie he'd seen. It was a Villa player. Ottilie had always liked to wear claret and blue, even though she'd no interest in Villa. He'd met her when she was wearing a claret and blue dress, fifty years ago. Her dress was one of the things that had attracted him to her. That, and Ottilie had been a looker. And she'd continued to be a looker right up until she drank her foxglove cup of tea. He could always count on Ottilie to give him something attractive to look at about the house. Still, she'd had to go. Even in dying she'd looked attractive, all made-up, her hair brushed back perfectly, not a strand out of place. She'd looked at him, clutching her chest, like she should've been in a picture, the kind of picture they used to show at The Roxie before they bulldozed it down for a car park. She hadn't said a word, experiencing her last moments. But the look on her face spoke a thousand words. She knew that he was her murderer. He could see it in her eyes, in her smile. She was as clever as clever came. That smile! It was as though she knew something that he didn't know. Then she'd flopped forward at the kitchen table, her face falling into her bowl of cornflakes, pasteurised milk streaking her brunette dye job. At their wedding, they'd both said they'd stay married to each other until death did them part. Ottilie had meant it, he knew. He'd meant it too, he knew. Though after a while, after fifty years—wasn't that time enough? Shouldn't one of them be dead already? 'Till death do us part' was all very well, but surely there should be a time limit, some kind of small print in the marriage certificate saying that if after fifty years either the bride or groom hadn't died, one or the other had freedom to end the marriage with a cup of foxglove tea? Well, as there wasn't—he'd cleverly written in the small print himself. He'd always loved Ottilie, in spite of her ruining his Saturdays. God only knew, he'd annoyed Ottilie, too; probably more, he'd say. Fifty years, though—fifty years! They would never have divorced. They weren't the type. The marriage would've gone on and on, interminably on. A cup of foxglove tea it had to be. Murder it had to be.

There was a painting hanging on the wall of a farmhouse pressed down with snow that Ottilie and he had bought at a flea market. They'd both played in the snow when it had snowed. There was the cracked floor tile that Ottilie and he had always meant to replace, but had never found the time. There were always funner things to do. And there were Ottilie's claret gardening wellies next to the kitchen door that he'd bought her one Christmas. Ottilie had kissed him and said they were just what she was after. His eyes were all right. He could see those things and they were those things, the same as they ever were. The painting was the painting. The cracked floor tile was the cracked floor tile. And the wellies were the wellies. He'd walk back to the kitchen table and sit down and pick up the paper and there would be a Villa player staring at him from the back page, and not Ottilie. The paper would be the paper. That's all there was to it.

Wilfred let go of the cooker and walked to the kitchen table, his bony feet ensconced in slippers, his footsteps hushed, a murderer's walk. He sat down at the kitchen table. Perhaps he should eat a bit more black pudding to settle his nerves? Ottilie would rather have let rain into the house than black pudding. "I'm not having black pudding in the fridge," she'd said. "What are you—a vampire?" Ah, vampires! They'd watched many Hammer horror movies on the tele together throughout the years, and those with Christopher Lee as Dracula had been their favourites. Sometimes in a tense moment, when Dracula was about to sink his fangs into another buxom beauty, Wilfred had become a vampire himself, suddenly nibbling Otillie's neck, catching her by surprise. And she'd laugh, and say, "Get away you silly bugger." Those had been fun evenings. He picked up his fork, pronged a lump of black pudding, and put it into his mouth. As good as the black pudding tasted, it didn't taste as good as Ottilie's neck. And Ottilie's foxglove tea hadn't tasted as good as her favourite hibiscus tea, that was for certain. He looked at the rest of his fry-up, all of it going cold on the plate. He could heat it up in the microwave later, after the Villa match. It wouldn't be as good, but he couldn't find his appetite, not with the paper on the table, not checking to see if his eyes were all right, when he knew his eyes were all right—weren't they?

Wilfred put his fork down on the plate and picked up the newspaper, his fingers trembling somewhat. The front page story was all about an American tourist getting stuck on Spaghetti Junction, going around and around unable to get off, and now they were suing the City of Birmingham for ruining their holiday. Why they had decided to have their holiday in Birmingham was beyond him. Wasn't Disney

World just down the road from them? Above that story, up in the top right hand corner of the paper, was the small headline: *Brum Derby: Back Pages Special!* His eyes were all right. He'd flip from the front page to the back page of the paper and read all about the Brum Derby—Villa against City. And there'd he see a photo of a Villa player, and not Ottilie. Yes, beyond a doubt, his eyes were all right. He flipped the paper, and there again he saw the same black and white photo of Ottilie—not, he was sorry to acknowledge, a Villa player. Once more he looked at the painting, the chipped floor tile, the wellies, and saw everything as it should be, as it ever was. Once more, he looked at the back page of the paper and saw the same black and white photo of Ottilie. Curse his all-right eyes! All being said and done, he'd rather his eyes were on the fritz than have Ottilie staring back at him from the back page of the paper. His mind went to the races, stuttering into a slow trot that picked up to a canter where it stayed, constant, never reaching the galloping speeds of his youth. What had she been up to, his cleverest Ottilie?

Ah, that photo! Wilfred knew it well. He'd taken it—what, forty years ago now? They'd been on their annual holiday to Blackpool. Ottilie had bought him a camera for his birthday the month previous, and out and about on Blackpool pier, with the Tower looming large and splendid in background, had been the first time he'd really got to try it out. Ottilie had always loved that photo of herself. He'd loved that photo of Ottilie, too. It was silver-framed and up on the sideboard in the living room. That would have to be put away with the urn in the cupboard under the stairs with the suitcases and spiders, too. "I look like a movie star in that photo," Ottilie had said often, passing the silver-framed photo, admiring her silver-screen looks. She'd always looked like a movie star—though he'd never told her; he couldn't find it within himself to tell her—even going to bed with her face white as a sheet, smothered in thick, anti-aging cream, as though she'd seen a ghost. Ottilie *was* a ghost now, there on the back page of the paper, her perfectly made-up eyes boring into him, stirring up memories that he didn't particularly want inside of his head on this Saturday—a Saturday that was supposed to have been *his* Saturday, not Ottilie's Saturday, as all the Saturdays had been before. One memory that rose higher than the others, demanding attention, was something Ottilie had said once, years back, and that had been that the only time she'd ever appear in the newspaper was after she'd died—on the obituary page. She'd said so after the time her tulips didn't win a prize at the library spring flower competition. She'd been that disappointed, that aggrieved, she'd gone to bed at six o'clock with a pile of Agatha Christie novels. Yes, the obituary page was for her, she'd said; to appear elsewhere meant you'd done something good, or you'd been up to no good, and she wasn't made of the necessary cloth for either.

Wilfred shivered as a cold sweat broke out over his wrinkled skin beneath his claret and blue striped pyjamas. Was this Ottilie's obituary? But it wasn't the obituary page. It was the back page of the paper, and the back page of the paper and those pages behind it were reserved for sports stories, and on Saturday morning reserved for football stories, and on a Saturday morning, when there was a derby being played later, reserved for stories about Villa, and City, too, but stories about City were just a waste of space and ink. The people at the paper should've known better. Though, as plain as day, there wasn't a story about the Villa-City game in sight, only a large black and white photo of Ottilie and a long column of newsprint that began with her name, big and bolded, as though it was the title of a picture up on the marquee of the old Roxie. ***Ottilie Rossiter***, the picture was called. And there was a long write-up to go along with it for all those to read with their Saturday morning breakfast. What with all the other arrangements he'd had to make the last few weeks—was it any wonder he'd forgotten about putting an obituary for Ottilie in the paper? If he'd made the arrangement, he would've ensured that the obituary would've appeared on the obituary page—on a Wednesday, say—where it was meant to be, not on the back page of the paper where it had no right to be, especially on the Saturday of the big match. But somehow, indubitably clever Ottilie had arranged it for herself, or with the help of someone else. So it didn't matter that he'd forgotten, did it? He looked from the paper to Ottilie's urn on the kitchen table next to the pot of tea. "What have you gone and done?" he asked, and then waited in silence, staring at the urn, and it was a nice urn, not the best money could buy, but not the worst either; it was a respectable-looking urn, one you wouldn't mind putting on a mantle for display, or a kitchen table for that matter. He half-expected Ottilie to answer him from inside of the urn, saying: "Read and find out." He wouldn't have put it past her to say something either. She'd always liked to have the last word. She'd joke occasionally, he now remembered, too, that if she were the first to die, she'd find a way to come back and visit him, if there was a way of coming back. Just to say hello, keep him on his toes and the like. He always used to shut her up with that kind of talk. He didn't like the idea of a ghost in the house. The idea of ghosts *at all*. He didn't want the house to be haunted, especially by the ghost of Ottilie. It was bad enough living with the rising damp. No, when you were dead, you were dead—and that was it, end of story. Let the living live in peace, and the dead keep out of the living's business, ashes in an urn.

Ottilie had always boxed cleverly, winning in the first round. He'd never been any match for her, until the twelfth round with a cup of foxglove tea. What had she written about her life, her marriage to him for fifty years? What couple these days would stay married for fifty years? People were divorcing more than the weather changed. It's sunny out, it would be a beautiful day to start divorce proceedings. Those rain clouds mean you'll be hearing from my solicitor in the morning. Hadn't their marriage been a good marriage all told, for those fifty years? He thought so. They'd had their ups and, of course, their downs. But that's the way marriage was—a Blackpool rollercoaster ride, every day of the week, Sunday through Monday. Saturdays, especially. Then there may come a time, after fifty years of marriage—for foxglove tea. And what is a person supposed to do when that time comes around? Foxglove tea is served, that's the order of the day. Bless Ottilie for her garden and her foxglove and her Agatha Christie novels. There was a solution for everything if you were one for keeping your eyes and ears open, and that solution could be sometimes right under your nose—or growing out in the back garden, a flower, tall and pink-purple, kind of like the pink-purple Ottilie had once dyed her hair. He hadn't liked the colour; he'd preferred Ottilie, the brunette she was born, but even with pink-purple hair she'd still looked like a movie star. He bet that even inside of the urn, she was a better-looking pile of ashes than there had ever been a pile of ashes, waiting for a camera to take a photo. It would be a photo worthy of a silver frame to be put up on a sideboard in the living room. He'd hadn't looked inside of the urn to see, though. He didn't have the nerve. Besides, people didn't go around lifting the lids from coffins to see what was inside a week after the burial, did they?—Well, except in the Hammer movies Ottilie and he used to watch on the tele—so it shouldn't be so for an urn. He wasn't a peeping Tom. A graverobber. But he *was* a murderer. The murderer who had done away with Ottilie. And there was Ottilie's obituary on the back of the newspaper, for him to read. Though not just him. Everyone! Right now, across Birmingham, people were sitting down to their breakfast with the same paper. They, too, were probably wondering what had happened to their back page. "What's this all about then? Who is this Ottilie? Was she somebody important?" they would ask. "She does look like a movie star. No, really, this is a scandal. An obituary should be on the obituaries page, not the back page. Where are my Villa players? City players even? I want to read about the match! Well, I don't know what to do. I'm all discombobulated. But if that's what you want me to read about—this Ottilie dying—I'll read about it. But I don't have to like it!"

The thought of other people about town sitting at their breakfast tables, reading Ottilie's obituary before he read Ottilie's obituary, was too much for Wilfred. He had to know first what Ottilie had written. Though then there came a knocking at his front door. He put down the paper. Who was that at this hour? Hadn't this Saturday brought him enough stress already! He wasn't expecting a caller. He didn't want a caller. He was still in his pyjamas. Why didn't they stop knocking? His ears weren't as good as his eyes, but he heard them knocking the first time. He'd heard the first time. What was with all the knocking? Were they trying to break down his front door? He heard a great thud, wood splintering, glass cracking. They were trying to break the door down! They had broken the front door down! What were they after? He didn't have anything worth stealing. They'd see the rising damp and know there wasn't anything worth stealing! What should he do? Ottilie would've known what to do. He could always rely on Ottilie to know what to do. She was the clever one. There she was—there in the urn, the urn rocking from side to side—his eyes were all right—rocking from side to side like the way Ottilie used to rock from side when she used to laugh. He'd always liked to see Ottilie laugh; she'd always laughed like it was going to be the last time for laughter in her life, so she'd laugh until there was no more laughter inside of her. And the laughter was loud like the authoritative voices he heard, getting closer and louder, and among those voices he heard the voice of Ottilie's sister Gertrude, too. Once you heard that voice, you never forgot that voice. What was Gertrude doing here? Shouldn't she be dying in Coventry? What had Ottilie gone and done? What had *he* gone and done? All he wanted were his Saturdays—this Saturday. Had that been too much to ask for after fifty years? He picked up the paper to read Ottilie's obituary...

Also by Daz Eek

Daz Eek is also the author of *The Crows That Ate Sunday* and *Two Knocks For Arthur*.

Buy directly from Daz Eek at https://dazeek.com/.